MIRAGE FOR PLANET X

By
STANLEY MULLEN

I0541457

ARMCHAIR FICTION
PO Box 4369, Medford, Oregon 97504

*For more information about Armchair Books and products, visit our
website at…*

www.armchairfiction.com

Or email us at…

armchairfiction@yahoo.com

INTERPLANETARY INTRIGUE AT ITS BEST

Torry had come to Mars looking for a man named Roper. They had been partners once—until Torry had found out what kind of man his partner really was. So with revenge and more on his mind, Torry set out for a public auction, an auction that featured two pieces of merchandise that would soon bring the worst elements of the Solar System into a showdown of frenzied bidding. The prize was sealed in two crates, its contents unknown. Yet scavengers from a dozen barbaric Moons; adventurers from nameless, semi-explored asteroids, arrived for the deathless auction…to bid on Roper's mysterious crates, the contents of which held the promise of a massive interplanetary confidence job, or the key to salvation for a dying race of people.

FOR A COMPLETE SECOND NOVEL, TURN TO PAGE 71

CAST OF CHARACTERS

TORRY

He came to Mars looking to even the score with a clever con man and hardened criminal—but there was much more to it than that.

THAROL SEN

She was beautiful in that blindingly exotic Martian way, and she was also blindingly loyal to a scoundrel from Earth.

GRANNAR

He was a tough, honest cop on a planet filled with corruption and the bitter remnants of a dying race.

BART ROPER

He'd made an amazing escape from an interplanetary prison to undertake a staggering interplanetary swindle.

SEN BAS

Dealing with a sly, brilliant criminal was something he was willing to do if it meant helping the people of his dying race.

FERAX

This repulsive Martian labor racketeer desperately wanted the contents of two unclaimed crates up for public auction.

CHAPTER ONE

THEY were bringing in the prisoners who had escaped from Phobos. Sand skimmer ambulances had raced to the spaceport outside the terraced Martian city and waited. Dust devils danced on the wide, wind-whipped Martian plains. Grannar of the Police and his silent companion examined each body as it was lowered from the rescue ship.

Death anywhere is an ugly business. On Mars, you get used to bodies that never rot. Deep-freeze temperatures hold down decay bacteria, and the dry, cold air quickly desiccates the tissue. Bodies turn into mummies that look and weigh like so much shredded wheat. But these corpses were worse—they were meaningless parodies that might never have been men. In primal disgust, Torry studied each one in turn, then shuddered and shook his head.

Grannar was tough minded, or stronger stomached. Police routines had taught him not to shudder.

"You can get used to this," he observed, enjoying Torry's revulsion. "Since you'd known Roper, we thought you could help us identify him. Thanks for coming along."

"Had I a choice?" asked Torry bitterly.

The policeman's laugh was brutal, explosive. "There is always a choice. You can do as you're told or be dragged in screaming."

Torry grimaced. "Much more of this and I'll be dragged out screaming."

The prisoner-escapees, what was left of them, were an unpleasant sight. Explosive decompression in airless space does curious things to men's bodies. Blood boils in the veins and flesh bursts from internal pressures. Also, there are heat-cold curiosities, with half a body burnt raw on the sunward side, and the rest frozen iron-hard with a lacy overlay of snowflake patterns in red.

Holden was still alive, by a miracle. Forward compartments had held together when the makeshift spacer blew its flimsy self inside out. He was alive but not talking. They brought the bulging mass of pulped, purple flesh back to Mars and dumped it in a basket. There was no face, no eyes, no recognizable hands or feet. For the time that remained to him, Holden would be less than a functioning animal, fed by tube, cared for by people he could not see or hear, living a precarious existence on the raw, black fringe of life. Holden was through talking. And for any practical purpose, through living.

"Too bad," said Grannar, looking into the basket. "He could have told us about a lot of things...if he'd wanted to."

"Holden was a nice guy before he knew Bart Roper," Torry snapped angrily.

"You sound pretty bitter about Roper."

"I should be. I know him better than you do. I am bitter about Roper."

"Because of Holden?" pressed Grannar.

"Not...Holden. But it might as easily have been me in that basket. Six years ago I was Roper's partner. I got out quickly when I found out some of his business methods. And I had very little he could steal from me then. A lot of people have a variety of good reasons to hate Roper. Just say that I'm one of them."

Grannar whistled a Martian tune. The sound was shrill and eerie in the thin air.

"You may as well ride back to the city in the police car with me," he suggested. "We can talk—"

"Talk!" blurted Torry. He swore savagely. "All this ugly business for nothing. You haven't found Roper yet. You don't even know if he made good his escape from your prison moon. In short, you don't know anything."

"True, up to a point," agreed the policeman quietly. "There are always many things I don't know. So I concentrate on the few things I do know. For example, you're very much interested in finding Roper. I'm wondering why. You can tell me about that on our way back to the city. About Roper himself, I know a few minor facts. Nobody has ever escaped from Phobos, the prison moon, but Roper may have managed it. With outside help he got materials and fittings smuggled in to construct a scratch spacer. It blew up, as we know, but Roper may have expected that. In a good spacesuit, he could have survived. Since we still haven't found him, dead or alive, he's probably circling somewhere in a private orbit, waiting to be picked up."

"It could be a long wait. One man is hard to find in all that space."

"Not necessarily. A code transmitter powered by transuranic alloys would keep sending indefinitely. And Roper could have agreed upon being picked up at some point of a fixed orbit by his outside friends. We'll find him, I think. In the meantime, we have you...and some questions. Wait in my car. I'll be with you as soon as I thumbprint some papers."

TORRY stumbled across the barren sand wastes of the spaceport, pitted or glazed here and there by old take-off blasts. Without trouble he located the half-track vehicle bearing police insignia. He got in and settled himself sourly to await Grannar's probing third degree. He meditated grimly on Roper, himself, and his reasons for coming to Mars…

Had it only been last night he arrived? It seemed eternities ago. Coming in from Earth by short orbit express, green with deceleration sickness, he had wondered why he was in such a rush. After four years a cold trail would not get any colder. It had not, of course. It was hot when he arrived and had been getting hotter by the minute. Only the fact of being aboard the express at the time of the prison break had cleared him in Grannar's eyes of being involved physically. And even that alibi did not erase suspicion from Grannar's suspicious nature.

Grannar was shrewd and deadly, a born hunter of men. Since the Martians never trust each other, most of the policing is done by hirelings from other planets. Grannar was an Earthman originally. But he was a long way from home, and twenty years on Mars had made him more Martian than the natives. He was hard, smart, dangerous, and a tough man to fool.

Torry had learned that at once last night.

But Grannar's return to the police car cut short his reverie. Torry watched the official cross the spaceport toward him, impressed by the lithe grace and sureness of movement over treacherous sand. Mars does something to a man who stays there. The body dries up and the soul withers, but if he survives, a man grows into something lean and leathery with pantherish strength and easy, poised motions.

Grannar vaulted to the driver's seat and slammed on power. With a skid of steering runners, the half-track took off toward the bubble city of New Chicago, named without tenderness by some long forgotten exile. Grannar drove with careless violence, but the half-track skimmer shot among the dunes and low, lichen-clad hills without incident.

There is no truth to the charge that it takes as long to get from the spaceport to New Chicago as it does to reach Mars from Earth. But the distance is impressive and the going rough. Grannar talked as he drove, seeming casual, but his questioning had the same icy skill and unerring judgment.

"We'll start at the beginning," he said.

"There is no beginning," Torry jerked out angrily. "I got in last night. Fresh from the spaceport and customs, I put a coin in the public visiphone and asked Central Information about Roper. Central had no information and returned my coin. It was a police trap. Your men picked me up, searched me with a Geiger counter and found the coin. You keep faintly radioactive coins in the visiphone machines for Central to return when someone is curious about police business. It came out even. You found out I was curious about Roper, and I found out he is police business, and his case is current. Do you think I'd be fool enough to call such attention to myself if I knew about Roper's prison break?"

"You might be. And it might be smart. That way you'd find out what the police knew and what they were doing. And it could be an alibi in case the breakout was delayed. We'll skip those possibilities for now. You were mulish last night about certain questions. I'm still not clear about why you are so desperate to find Roper. Why?"

Torry smiled coldly. "That's easy. I have to find him for a legal release. Preferably dead, which will make things easier for everybody. But if he's alive, I want his signature and prints on some papers."

"Why? What papers?"

Torry hesitated. "It's a touchy subject. A personal matter. Nothing to do with the police."

"I'll be the judge of that. Keep talking."

"Have you ever spent five years on an asteroid all by yourself?"

Grannar grunted. "Fortunately not. Twenty years on Mars is bad enough for me. Have you?"

Torry's face twisted in bitterness. "I have. I cracked up my one-man spacecan while prospecting in the asteroids. I was there five years until a survey ship happened by. There were minerals, low-grade transuranics, but good enough to work when you had nothing else to do. I worked out the whole asteroid and had a good payload for the survey ship when it brought me back. Not a big fortune, but a stake that looked pretty good to me. I'm not rich now, but I can get along without skipping meals."

"What's the connection with Roper?"

"None in that part of it. I went prospecting after I'd dissolved my partnership with Roper. Times were bad, and I couldn't tie up with a decent job. There was a girl—"

"There usually is. Who was she?"

"Rose Mead, then. She promised to wait for me. She didn't. She's Roper's wife now. Not that I blame her too much. A year can be a long time, and five years is longer when you're a castaway on a small asteroid. Nothing to look at but a sky full of stars. Nothing to breathe but hydroponic-cycle air. No food but your homemade synthetics and the green stuff you grow in your chemical vats. You work and eat and sleep, and any idea can become an obsession. Sometimes it's one woman, sometimes an imaginary harem. I had a 3-D picture of Rose. It helped to hold me together, or maybe it just channeled an idea that was bound to go haywire."

"You're beginning to make sense," commented Grannar. "So you have an obsession about Roper's wife?"

"I call it that. But I figure that all my money is not worth much if it won't buy just one thing I've dreamed about for five long years. There's a technicality about divorcing a man who's away from Earth, in space. Rose is funny about it. But she's agreed that her marriage was a mistake. She'll marry me if I can prove Roper is dead, or can get a release from him."

"Is the girl worth all this trouble?"

TORRY grinned cynically. "Probably not. But Rose is a good, sound, practical minded girl. Maybe my money looks good to her. Roper left her four years ago with hardly any resources. For myself, after five years of dream stuff, a solid human girl like Rose looks pretty good. Dream stuff looks fragile, but it's mighty tough eating for a daily diet."

"So you want to find Roper. Preferably dead, you say. Does that include pushing him off a cliff if you find him?"

Torry snorted. "It could. That depends on Roper."

The policeman echoed the snort. "Roper is dangerous. You may have forgotten how tricky and ruthless he can be. Sounds to me like hunting a tiger with a butterfly net."

Torry smiled viciously. "Even that can be done...if the net is big enough and strong enough. I'm counting on a curious twist in Roper's mind. I'm a challenge to him—the one man so far he failed to swindle or corrupt. He pulled a fast one about Rose, but he knows I wasn't there to fight back. It galls him. And if he knows I'm here, alive, and looking for him, maybe he'll find me and try to wipe out the one flaw in his record."

Grannar shot a glance of grudging admiration, but shook his head. "At the moment, I wouldn't count on it. He'll be busy and we'll see to it that he is. But if you want to go looking for him, maybe I can help you."

"Do you know where he is?"

"No, but I can give you some hints where to look."

"Why?" Torry was baffled.

"Two reasons. Maybe more, but two will do. I'm a cop, so I hate men like Roper. If he's on Mars I'll get him sooner or later because I'm a good cop. And it's my job. I hate crooks, so I'll kill him or catch him and send him to Phobos for keeps. The second reason is that I hate Mars. It's a tough world—what government there is, is corrupt and vicious. Offend the wrong people or stir things up, and you're out without your pension. You can even get hurt. I want out while I'm still ahead, with enough money to go back to Earth and live decently. And so far I haven't that kind of money."

"I don't see the connection," protested Torry.

Grannar's bushy eyebrows crawled up and down like caterpillars.

"There's big money in this Roper business. There has to be for anyone to take the risk of arranging a breakout from Phobos—that costs plenty."

"Roper must have something pretty good this time to attract help like that. What is it?"

Grannar shrugged. "I don't know. My guess is transuranics—the heavy metals beyond uranium in the atomic table; the stuff that powers planets. Without it our whole economy breaks down, and we can't even afford to make air for places like Mars. But you've mined it yourself. You know how rare and valuable it is."

"I know," said Torry. "You think Roper has a new source?"

"Maybe that, and maybe he's discovered or stolen a cheaper way to process or transport it."

"It figures," admitted Torry. "Roper was always interested in transuranics, and always looking for a squeeze play like that. He'd be able to make his own terms, wouldn't he? Including squaring the charges against him?"

"Just about any terms he dictated," grated the detective.

"Why tell me this?"

Grannar's eyes narrowed. "You want Roper for your own good reasons. I want him for mine. My hands are tied but yours are not. If you want him, go after him. I'll help, short of risking my job. I'm offering to make a deal with you. It occurs to me that a couple of smart men could make a real killing by knowing the right time to buy a few shares of stock in transuranics. A man like me might even make enough to retire to Earth, comfortably."

"You're beginning to make sense," said Torry. "What makes you so sure I'll cut you in for a slice?"

Grannar laughed harshly. "My nuisance value; for one thing. My usefulness for another. I'm an honest cop. But there's nothing in the rulebook that says I can't pick up valuable information on the side while I'm doing my job. And nothing that says I can't put pressure on you to help me do it. Besides, why should you balk at doing me a favor when you're doing yourself one at the same time?"

"I'm still listening."

"New to Mars, aren't you?"

"New enough. I've been here before, but a long time ago and not for long then. Why?"

"Do you know anything about the local set-up, the governments?"

"Not much. It's a kind of anarchy, I think. The big companies and even the labor racketeers have private armies like the old goon squads. Legal government is just a front for feudal gangs, with the police sitting politely on the lid. Lobbies and pressure groups are the real bosses. Is that right?"

GRANNAR whistled his aimless Martian tune. "You said it. I didn't. Not out loud. I never even think it in a room that might have microphones or scanners. Mars is interesting, beautiful, with shreds and tatters of an old, picturesque culture clinging to ivy-patterns to the new, modern, cosmopolitan, industrial set-up. It says that in the books and travel ads. Out here in the clean and lifeless air of a worn-out planet I can have the precarious luxury of hating it. I want out, and you're going to help me get out."

"Why stay anyhow?"

"Because I'm a cop and it's the only job I know. And bad as it is, it's better than nothing. You've heard the yarn of the brash young rookie in Earth's Sahara City, the guy famous for arresting the police commissioner's daughter. I'm that cop. I hung a ticket on her for traffic violation. It turned out she was drunk and speeding away from an accident that killed somebody. The mess was too ugly to hush up, so she went to prison and I went to the sticks for keeps. I resigned and came here. So I learned to keep my mouth shut, do as I was told, and never to move an inch out of line with the people who count."

"You're breaking my heart," Torry said bitterly. "Go on."

"Roper's not alone in this. Somebody with money and political influence arranged that escape, probably picked him up off the wreck. Before he went to Phobos he was mixed up with Trans-Uranic Miners Union, and also with a Martian pressure group headed by old Sen Bas, the importer. He may still be. I want no trouble with either. With you it doesn't matter. Maybe you'll dig up a lot of interesting facts before you get yourself killed."

"Get to the point."

"Spacefreight. Two large boxes consigned to Roper and Holden, his partner. Still unopened, held in the unclaimed spacefreight warehouse. Charges are high and Roper was broke. He tried to get money from Trans-U and the Martians, but neither was buying a pig in a poke. Not then. Maybe they are now. He must have convinced his backers, somehow. But they can't get the space crates either unless I say so. Roper and his pal tried robbery to raise money and landed on Phobos. I put the crates under police seal."

"Why weren't they condemned and opened?"

"Too much red tape and money. The transport company can sell the stuff legally for charges, but only at public auction, unopened, and bids start at charges plus storage. Are you interested?"

Torry frowned. "My funds are not unlimited…"

"That's a chance we'll both have to take. I'm taking a chance on you anyhow, but don't try any smart tricks. I always cover bets. The boxes will be officially released for tomorrow's auction. All I ask is a look inside at Roper's gimmick, whatever it is, so I'll know whether to buy transuranics or not. If you buy the boxes the contents are yours. Fair enough?"

Torry grunted. "If they sell low enough you'll get your look after I've had mine."

"See that I do," warned Grannar. "And a word of advice. You can't import weapons to Mars, but there's no law says you can't buy one here and sleep with it. Shall I drop you at your hotel?"

The half-track was nearing the domed city. A gigantic half bubble of polarized plastic rose from the plain to enclose both the old Martian town and the bustling, strident metropolis of New Chicago. From the desert the dome was nearly invisible, but the architectural jumbles looked like a forest of lighted Christmas trees appearing by magic in the swift dusk of the red planet.

Torry grinned. "You're forgetting I spent my first night in jail."

Grannar scoffed. "Routine, one in jail, one in a hotel, the next in the morgue…"

CHAPTER TWO

AN AUCTION of unclaimed, refused or damaged spacefreight held more surprises and excitements than a Martian wedding. All shipments were sold "as is, unopened," which offered endless possibilities to a daring purchaser.

Anything could pop out of a sealed space crate when the container was broken into, and sometimes it did, literally. One unlucky bidder got, seven full-grown grull cats, shipped from Venus in suspended animation. His purchase caused seven minor riots until company guards with gas guns could subdue the savage killers. Loot from a dozen inhabited worlds and a hundred half-explored moons and asteroids littered the floor or spilled from damaged cases.

Bids ran high and two dozen small fortunes changed hands as Lots 1 to 24 went up at auction and were knocked down. Any bid on unclaimed freight was a gamble, a big gamble, and it was one of the rare things not taxed to death by a greedy government. And the inhabitants of New Chicago were gamblers, or they would not have been there. The crowd was mixed and polyglot—human and half-human species rubbed elbows and tempers to a fine frenzy.

"Lot 25," sang the auctioneer. "Who'll open?"

To avoid attracting attention, Torry had bid half-heartedly on several previous items, breathing a sigh of relief when bids pyramided and the lots sold to someone else.

This time, he merely sparked off the bidding, only to have a Martian importer jump down his throat with an offer of twice the amount. Torry dropped out as the bidding climbed in dizzy spirals, and the shipment went to the impatient Martian for the price of a small spaceline. Laughter rippled over the auction lofts as the boxes were opened and found to contain forty small air conditioners of a type useless on Mars.

Lot 26 sold badly after that disappointment. It proved to be a treasure of rare luminous birds from Venus, and collectors immediately offered the fortunate purchaser triple his money for the lot.

"Lot 27," roared the auctioneer before excitement could die down. "Two large boxes to be sold separately. No information on these...except that they were held overtime in storage and have just been released from police seal. The space crates are undamaged. Who'll open?"

Torry felt like a small child back on Earth, clutching moist bronze pennies in his hot, grimy fist as he ran to the corner candy store. Nerves and muscles contracted in his throat. He opened his mouth but no sound came out.

"Fifty credits," shouted the Martian who had bought Lot 25. "I want to recoup my losses," He stared belligerently at Torry.

Somebody else doubled the bid.

Torry found a shadow of his voice and redoubled. Grinning evilly, the Martian raised again, but not before he shot a wary glance across the room. Torry met the challenge, then following the direction of the Martian's glance, he spotted a Martian girl standing near the doorway. She was so swathed in blue Venusian spidersilk as to be practically invisible, and there was time for only a general impression. But Torry did not miss the head-nod signal, instructing the Martian male to bid for her. After the man's previous performance, Torry braced himself for spirited competition.

Up and up went the bids...astronomically.

At twenty thousand credits the Martian hesitated for an automatic mute appeal to the feminine figure. The girl nodded again, but that moment's doubt cost the Martian.

"...Third and last time. Sold to the Earthman...for twenty thousand credits."

Torry swallowed hard. He saw the girl glide toward him through the crowd, moving as smoothly and silently as a ghost.

Like a maniac the Martian charged to the platform, croaking a loud protest. Arguments became heated, voices were raised in harsh clamor, then blows struck. Grinning, Torry watched the scramble. A knot of uniformed company guards surged around the battling Martian and hustled him from the auction rooms. A gas gun was used finally to subdue the raging sportsman. While Torry waited for attendants to bring him the box and his purchase receipts, he looked again for the girl but she had melted into the crowd.

Interest was now roused to a high pitch. The auctioneer went into his spiel in whatever alien language auctioneers use, and it was only by knowing in advance what was being said that anyone could make sense of the garble.

"...Other half of Lot 27," droned the husky voice. "How about a thousand credits to open?"

"One thousand," Torry bid hoarsely.

He felt sweaty and feverish at the same time. Mentally he calculated his remaining resources. A little more of this and the show would be out of his price class.

Bidding was rapid. In jumps the price went up from twenty to thirty thousand. The Martian's hysteria seemed to have infected everyone. At thirty-five thousand, bidding slowed.

"Thirty-six thousand," Torry bid.

Moments lengthened and Torry's breath came slowly back. It was the absolute limit of his available cash, and the auction terms were cash on the spot. Numbly, he realized that his bid, if it were accepted, used up more than half of his fortune from five years of lonely work.

"Thirty-seven thousand," offered a bull-throated voice. And a barrel-bodied mine owner from Iobololy thrust himself forward as if to give authority to his bid.

Torry had shot his wad. He could not raise the bid, and it meant loss of the second box. Slowly, the starch dissolved out of him and he let his excitement wilt.

With bidding so high, the auctioneer was not impatient. He studied Torry hopefully. The moment extended. The gavel raised, slammed down.

"Going once."

A thrusting hand delved into Torry's pocket where he clutched grimly at his sheaf of paper credits. For an awful moment he thought his pocket was being picked. Then crisp, rustling paper bulged his pocket, and realization bulged his eyes. There was no time for thought or argument. In blind confusion, he drew out a packet of paper money and stared at it. A cruel fist jabbed into Torry's ribs.

"Going twice…at thirty-seven thousand."

"Forty thousand!" screamed Torry.

Bids climbed again, to fifty thousand, to fifty-five, then to sixty. At sixty-two thousand, the fat man from Io gave up.

"Sold," droned the auctioneer. "I hope the man from Earth has the money, and his money's worth. Now, Lot 28, five cases, one broken open. The rest…"

Torry did not hear any more. He turned and stared blankly at a vision in blue spidersilk. Gossamer fabric so swathed the girl, covering so densely in so many folds, that she had no more form than an ear of corn. A face showed dimly through layers of diaphanous cloth, but no features were clear enough to have real definition.

"Who are you?" gasped Torry.

"Your partner." The voice, as smooth and silken as the garments, seemed bodiless, but it suggested purringly that the girl was not. "Don't be so obvious about it. We won't open the boxes here. Hire men to move our loot and I'll have a robotruck waiting outside the freight doors in five minutes. Be there."

Torry nodded dumbly. She vanished again, so quickly that he almost wondered if he had imagined her. But her money was real enough. He fumbled it, paying grim-faced attendants, then hired men to move the heavy crates to the freight elevator. At street level, with the boxes blocking most of the entrance, he waited.

A wheeled robotruck quickly appeared and the girl descended the ramp. Like a blue fury, she directed the men and had the space crates loaded in a brace of minutes. Then a hand snaked out from the fabric folds.

"Half of eighty-two thousand is forty-one thousand," she said. "We can settle up now."

"Half of sixty-two thousand," objected Torry.

"You don't know me very well," she murmured. "It has to be all or nothing."

The gun against his stomach decided Torry. "Don't be like that. You win." He shrugged. "I guess we're both taking a chance at that. Forty-one thousand is a heavy investment in curiosity."

The gun vanished. "You've no idea how much of a chance we're taking," she mused aloud. "People are curious. Yo Tyal is a fool, and I didn't dare attract attention by bidding myself. Half of the Trans-U Miners' goon squad was at that auction just watching me. You should know what that means."

"Should I?"

"You should. If you don't…but we can't stand here talking like moonstruck lovers. Not unless we're tired of living. Which is it, partner, me or the goon squad?"

"You, I guess," Torry laughed grimly. "Though if I'd known about the goon squad I'd have given you less argument."

Her head tossed under the myriad veilings of spidersilk. She scrambled aboard the robotruck and pressed the motor stud. "Come on, then," she ordered sharply.

The truck was in motion almost before Torry could leap to the seat beside her.

Going at suicidal speed through the twisting alleyways of the old city, Torry felt hopelessly confused and lost. Worse, the girl kept glancing over her shoulder, and her driving suffered. It was reckless enough at best.

"Keep your eyes on the road," Torry urged. "Unless you're psychic you can't watch where you're going and where we've just been. If anything's following us, it's probably just an ambulance looking for business."

"Make sure," she ordered breathlessly.

At first Torry could distinguish nothing but a blurred rush of shadowy buildings whirling away behind them as if being drawn toward some colossal whirlpool. But he sensed pursuit, just as the girl had, perhaps because she seemed to expect it. Then he saw two huge dark vehicles race into view just before she swerved the robotruck around a corner and shut off rear vision.

"We are being followed," he grudged. "Now where, partner?"

"Home, I had thought," she said. "But we'll never make it. And I don't want those wolves going through our place. It's bad enough without that."

THE robotruck hit a straight stretch. Pencil beams of light licked out from the street shadows behind. Fire flowers blossomed, but the noise of heavy explosions was lost in the roar of racing motors. Showers of dust and flakes of fiery, disintegrating masonry deluged the careening robotruck.

Hurtling around a blind corner, the truck aimed itself into a narrow opening between buildings. Metal ground and screamed in abrasive contact with stone but the robotruck rebounded and careened down side alleys, around sharp corners, and over moving walks fortunately deserted. With the nerveless skill of an old trucker, the girl wrestled some sanity into the vehicle and chose her route from the most unlikely possibilities. At last, after a sprint through a tangle of dark avenues and narrow alleys she brought the robotruck to a brake melting halt in the deep shadow of high, blank-faced buildings.

"See what I mean?" she said, voice loud and shrill in the silence that seemed deafening with the motor cut out.

Shuddering, the girl crouched behind the seat shield and fumbled inside her garment for the gun, alert for signs of pursuit.

"Relax," advised Torry. "We're alone for the moment. Wherever we are."

"It's an abandoned warehouse. Belongs to my grandfather," she gasped. "Can you get those boxes inside with only me to help?"

"Of course, if there's tackle, some wheels, and a ramp."

With a coded light-key the girl opened heavy doors and got necessary equipment. Fortunately, she was stronger than she looked, and about as fragile as steel wire. She gave Torry no more mercy than she gave herself. It was still a mean job.

Inside the vast, echoing interior, Torry and his companion seemed as unimpressive as ants in an auditorium. Huge, vaulted lofts were dusty with disuse. The huge cubes of the space crates looked like unmarked dice, rolled by giants, and forgotten.

Torry was tired and irritable. "I've played along with you," he said. "Now that we're here I'd like some facts. Because of the boxes, I'll assume you have a connection with Roper. Who are you, and what is all this about?"

"Don't you know?" demanded the girl. Laughing an icy trill, she threw back the veiling spidersilk from head and face, bunching the material neatly behind her neck. Her face was oddly elfin and distorted to curious proportions by the Martian half-mask of delicately etched glass. Wide set eyes of periwinkle blue tilted at the corners, and the smile of her sword-slash mouth was both teasing and disarming, Torry was suddenly glad that there had been no such face as hers to remember during his five-year exile.

"I'm Tharol Sen," she murmured. "My grandfather is Sen Bas, the Martian importer. Does that explain anything?"

"It may," said Torry, "but not to me. I'm a stranger here, myself. Long ago I was Roper's partner. We heard he was dead. You might say I'm acting for his estate."

"Roper is still alive, very much alive. And don't worry, he can look after his own affairs."

An ugly thought then struck Torry, though he had gnawed at the idea before. "You don't happen to be one of his affairs?"

Her smile vanished. The dark hair swirled like black smoke as she tossed her head. Her eyes turned dark and cold with the arrogant pride of her ancient race.

"That was a bad choice of words, partner," she said with a haughty stare. "I have promised to marry Bart Roper."

Anger surged hotly in Torry.

"Bad choice of words for you, not me. Roper can't marry you or anyone else. "Whatever arrangement you have—" He stopped. "Did he happen to mention a wife back on Earth?" He hoped the flash of resentment in him was for Rose, not for himself.

"Roper said she was dead," the girl answered. "Perhaps he believes she is dead. In any case, it doesn't matter. Martian law does not recognize marriages on other planets. He can pay her off and I'll see that he forgets her."

"Perhaps." Torry mastered himself. "I'd still like to know what I paid all those credits for."

"Why not open the boxes and find out?"

FROM a trapdoor locker she brought tools, an atomic torch and a huge wrecking bar. The boxes yielded easily to persuasion.

The first box, which was smaller, contained an assortment of lenses. Banks of atomic-electric batteries hooked up into an intricate arrangement of copper wire coils did not explain any puzzles. Nor did the contents of the larger case, which were mainly a folding framework of metal suspending endless layers of foil or metalcloth too finely woven for the eye to follow. The foil or fabric was eerie stuff, as unsubstantial as curdled moonlight. Like liquid mercury, it seemed almost alive as it crawled away from the touch.

"I thought the only mirages you could buy came in bottles," commented Torry unhappily.

"Don't be a fool," rasped the girl in a strange tone. "It is a mirage...for Planet X. I thought you knew more since you knew Roper. But I'll stand by my agreement. All or nothing, both ways. I'd better explain. And now that you're in, try to act intelligent. I'll tell you all I can, then we'd better get this equipment to...to my grandfather before anything else happens."

A buzzer near the metal sliding doors droned a warning. The girl's face turned upward toward a blinking red alarm light.

"I'd say something was already happening," said Torry.

"Someone's in the alley outside," gasped Tharol Sen. It can't be the police. They wouldn't dare interfere."

"Then who...?"

"Probably Ferax of Trans-U Miners Union. Or his strong-arm squad, if they find us here with...with that, they'll kill both of us. I don't know what to do."

"Why don't you stop fooling with that silly blaster gun? Give it to me and find yourself a hole to crawl in. This is my department. Let me do the worrying."

She laughed. "I might do just that." She handed over her popgun. It was a typical woman's weapon, squat, flat and short-barreled. Up close it could vaporize a man, but it would have no range worth mentioning. Torry grinned at it in contempt. Motioning her out of the line of fire, he crouched behind the wrecked crates.

A heavy crash echoed through the cavern-like vaults as force was applied to the metal doors, but the doors were duro-steel, two inches thick. They held, but the interior reverberated with harsh metallic clangor. Two more blows sounded—then a lengthening silence. A circle of redness glowed incandescent on the metal, spreading over the panels like spilled paint. Waves of heat sprang outward. Heat haze danced in the cool air as visible vibrations of blinding crimson radiated from the softening door. Runnels of melting steel channeled the metal surface, dripping to spatter on floor.

The girl was busy with something, but with his eyes riveted on the door, Torry could not spare her any attention. He imagined she might be trying to hide the contents of the boxes.

"They'll be through in a minute," she whispered.

Torry nodded. Drops of water splashed down suddenly. Torry felt it on hands and face, glanced upward. Rain, inside a building in a domed city! He must be crazy. But it was real. Drops became a deluge, slashing down in increasing torrents. Water sizzled on the incandescent door, and clouds of steam burst upward, obscuring everything. Pools formed, joined. In moments the floor was inches deep in water.

"Automatic sprinklers," said the girl. "Set for any upward shift of temperature."

Steam clouds cleared. A needle of light burned through. In rifts, Torry saw the door dissolve, slide suddenly into a bubbling, spitting mass that spread in fiery rush across the floor. In wild rush came dark figures, dancing gingerly to avoid tongues of hot metal. Torry fired carefully.

He kept finger on stud until the blaster charge was used up. He flung the useless weapon. But the dark figures were gone. The doorway, with sagging leaves of soft metal, was empty.

"That's all, sister," he said, turning.

She was gone. Something like a blue flash whisked out of vision. There was only the metal framework supporting a cylinder of the woven quicksilver. And, as he watched, it vanished.

More dark figures blocked the doorway. They came at him in a surge of reckless violence. He stood up and met them with empty hands. Then darkness struck through his brain.

CHAPTER THREE

TORRY opened one eye cautiously. He was in bed, a soft bed with clean linens. Beside the bed loomed a monstrous figure. Something that might have been, and was, a Venusian type-R mutant. It seemed not quite human, and big even for a Venusian. But it was not a stranger.

"Ferax…" whispered Torry, opening both eyes.

"It's been a longtime," said the Venusian in thick accents.

"Not long enough."

Ferax laughed brutally. His head was a hairless globe of coarse leather, into which some humorist had punched a parody of human features while the material was still pliable. Nothing about Ferax looked pliable now.

"You're still tough, Torry. And you're keeping fast company these days. But you'll never learn to work with your brain instead of your fists or a gun."

Torry smiled with bruised, pulpy lips. "Look who's talking. You're getting soft, Ferax. Last time your boys worked over Roper and me we couldn't walk or talk for a week. And I hear you're in fast company yourself since you gave up strikebreaking and took over union racketeering. You may be a big name now, but you're as ugly as ever. And to me, you'll always smell like the skunk in the perfume works."

Ferax bellowed happily. "Smells are more subtle in higher brackets, that's all. In a stinking world, nobody smells too pretty. Not even you, and certainly not your girl friend—or is she Roper's?"

"Tharol Sen? Roper's, I guess. You'll have to ask them. I barely saw the girl myself. I just got in night before last, spent a day answering questions for the police, then rested up one night before buying myself a package of trouble. Nobody tells me anything, so I'll have to guess. Is Roper behind this rat race?"

Ferax grunted. "I could almost believe you don't know. So I'll tell you. He's in with a Martian power grab. They need transuranic metals to power their underground cities. The stuff is scarce and expensive. Everyone's looking for new sources and we'll have to find some soon or our whole economy will break down. The Martians are in the same jam, desperate."

"Roper has a new source?"

"Not new. We all know where the metals are. Neptune's big moon, Triton. And Pluto. The trouble is getting them out."

Torry shook his head. "But you've mined under bad conditions before. Triton and Pluto should be no worse than some."

"Not the mining. Transportation. Freight rates from Pluto or Triton would eat up all the profits. And take too much time. Who wants to spend twelve years hauling in one shipload of ore? The answer is…nobody. The Martians can afford the money since they're already paying top rates for whatever we can supply. But we think Roper has a short cut for transportation—"

"If he has I'd better get in with him. Sounds like a very good profit…

Ferax chuckled. "I know better than that. You and Roper hate each other worse than you hate me. Besides, I can offer a better deal. He'll only swindle you out of your cut, and you know it. Throw in with me and you'll stay alive, plus a slice of whatever I take."

"Are you serious about that? If so, I'll have to think it over. Is there any use asking you where I can find Roper?"

"No use at all," said Ferax, grinning. "I don't know. If I did, I'd go there after him. If you do I'll have you followed. You always did have a genius for picking the losing side, which makes it a pleasure to fight you. You're free to go as soon as you're strong enough. If you decide to play things my way, let me know. I'll give you a pass, day or night. Getting into union headquarters is like breaking into the mint. I live like a minor king, and the place is a fort."

Torry snorted. "It's probably safer that way, when so many people hate your guts."

Ferax shrugged. "For that compliment I'll give you some free advice. Don't tell the police about that shooting fray in the warehouse. You're nobody, and the police would love to clear the union and your Martian twirp by using you for scapegoat. You or the girl killed six of my best hardheads. Also, if you see her or old Sen Bas, watch yourself. They're both trickier than snakes and a lot more poisonous."

"One thing more," said Torry. "What happened to the girl?"

Ferax opened eyes wide. "You tell me. She was gone, along with the stuff from the boxes. My men found you sprawled out unconscious from a blow on the head. You were suckered, friend. Suckered."

Ferax produced a metal ident card impregnated with coded electronic inks. "This will keep you out of jail if your cop friend has any such ideas. Also, it will get you in here to see me anytime, day or night, if you change your mind."

Torry laughed, but accepted the card uneasily. "That will be the day or night…"

LIKE all police stations, the building reeked of unwashed bodies and harsh disinfectants. In Grannar's office, Torry faced out the storm.

"Amateur!" said Grannar in disgust. "Why did I ever get mixed up with you?"

Torry glared back at him. "Our lovey-dovey arrangement is brittle enough to break off any time you want it that way."

Grannar shook himself like a wet dog. "Not yet. Whether you know it or not, you did pick up some interesting facts. I guess Tharol Sen has tricked smarter men than you. And she'll probably keep that partnership bargain, since Martians are funny about honor in a business deal. Since she was the one at the auction we can assume that the Martians picked up Roper from the wrecked escape ship and that he's alive."

"I'm sure she knows where Roper is," said Torry. "Now if I knew where to find her—"

"That's easy enough," Grannar told him acidly. "Her grandfather has a big place in the old Martian sector, about twenty acres on the surface and no one knows how many cubic miles of tunnels and cellars underground. He calls himself an importer, and after his own quaint way, he is. Any vice for a price. Sen Bas' Garden of Delights is a combination gambling den, freak show, amusement park, carnival and emporium of forbidden drugs and narcotic liquors. We've tried raiding the joint but gave that up. Too risky, with their mines and booby traps, and the

Martians just scamper into the holes and get lost. Below ground is a rabbit warren of caverns and tunnels and vaults that used to be for growing and curing mushrooms and commercial molds. We know the girl is there, somewhere, but—"

"But you're afraid to go in after her?"

"Not quite that. If ordered on regular police business I'd go poking into even that Martian hornet's nest. But we have nothing on her or Sen Bas, and only a suspicion that Roper's hiding there. Since you muffed something easy, like the auction, I doubt if you could manage to get in, let alone locate her or Roper."

"Who says I muffed anything?" demanded Torry irritably. "I know what was in the boxes, though I didn't tell the girl I knew. It's a matter transmitter, the only one in the Solar System. An inventor back on Earth was knocked on the head and his working model stolen. He's alive, but has lost his memory, and the plans were taken along with the model. Roper's big secret is stolen property, but getting it back may be a problem. I didn't guess what it was till the girl used it to escape from the warehouse. Probably they want the thing to bring back heavy metal ores from Triton or Pluto. I've learned more in three days than you did in four years."

Grannar bowed sardonically. "Oh, sure. I apologize. And now I'm sure you can lay hands on a man with a perfect escape method—from anywhere to anywhere. The rat holes were bad enough, but this really does it."

"The girl is still a good lead," said Torry quietly. "I'm going after her. Are you, or do I have to ask help from Ferax?"

"Suit yourself about Ferax. I won't risk my job on a chance Roper *might* be there—"

"How much is your job worth?" asked Torry, with a sneer.

Grannar's face twitched. "For half that dough you threw away at the auction, I could buy a plankton farm on Earth…"

Torry licked his lips and left. Back at the hotel he cashed a bank draft and put twenty thousand credits in currency into an envelope with a note and sent it to Grannar. The note began:

I've always wanted to buy a policeman. Now you can afford to do your job. I'm seeing Ferex first, but with or without his help, I'm going after Roper.

Terse instructions followed. Torry did not expect too much of Grannar, but the man represented law and authority as far as either existed on Mars, and dealing with Roper, Ferax, and the Martians all at once was scarcely a one-man job.

CHAPTER FOUR

TRANS-U MINERS UNION housed itself in a citadel remarkable even on Mars. It occupied the center of a large area, cleared, floodlighted, and surrounded by a charged wire fence. Inside the defense circle were booby traps triggered for the first careless step off marked pathways patrolled by robot guards. Torry's metal ident card got him through the gateway by tripping electronic relays and each incorruptible robot guard passed him after being shown the card.

At the building doorway he had to satisfy a series of dubious and hard bitten human questioners, but his pass and the magic name of Ferax got him inside.

Doors opened. Robot voices directed him across echoing lobbies to a bank of elevators. In a locked cage he descended five floors below surface level. In the corridor another bodiless voice spoke:

"End of the hall. Door on the right."

Torry followed directions. The ritual was getting on his nerves. His footsteps echoed hollowly. The place smelled damp and moldy as a tomb. Opening the door on the right with a wave of his keyed pass, he realized that it *was,* in a sense, a tomb. There was a body in it. A dead body.

Ferax sprawled across an ornate desk of Venusian chibar wood and kru-leather.

Luminous particles from a blaster discharge still danced in the air. A lingering bite of charred, exploding flesh stung the nostrils. There was little left of the torso, but a lolling globular head identified the corpse. A discarded gun clanked as Torry's foot kicked it. He hesitated, then picked it up and renewed the charge. It was an automatic reflex of defense, and fingerprint evidence was not likely to matter now. If found on the spot he would have little chance for explanations.

The thing had happened only minutes ago. Whoever did it, the killer must still be close at hand. A roving flicker of pale radiance warned Torry that a scanner was in use. By whom? From where? No complex mental processes were needed to convince Torry that he was in a bad spot. The goon squads were notorious for acting first and asking questions afterwards.

Getting into the citadel to see Ferax had been interesting enough. Getting out again promised to be more so. If he ever got out.

The office door was opening slowly. Silently Torry glided behind it. Reaching around it, he snatched cloth and flesh and dragged a struggling form into the room.

"Tharol Sen!"

The girl was panting, her periwinkle eyes wide and glazed with horror.

Torry subdued her writhings by jamming the blaster muzzle hard into her flesh.

"Talk low," he ordered. "But talk fast. Why did you kill Ferax?"

"I didn't. I found him like that, just a moment ago. I heard the blaster and looked in quickly. Then I hid in the office across. I heard something and came back here. That's all I know," Her voice ended on a wail.

Torry jerked up the elfin face and studied it savagely. For some reason he believed her. But there was more to explain, even if someone else had killed the labor racketeer, and little time for explanations.

"How did you get in here?" he snapped. "And why?"

She threw back her head in a characteristic gesture. Her eyes sparkled.

"Roper had come here. He was so long that I got worried. I came through. She stopped talking suddenly.

"Through the matter transmitter? I know about it, so you can call it by the right name."

Tharol Sen nodded numbly.

"That means Roper killed him."

The girl jerked angrily. "Bart Roper wouldn't do that. He wouldn't kill an unarmed man. Probably you killed him, and just want to throw the blame on...on us."

Torry ignored her. "Roper would be too smart to leave any evidence. So I'll leave it for him." From his pocket he took a small lighter with a name engraved on it, quickly scrubbed it free of prints and dropped it on the floor as if it had fallen in the excitement of murder. It would not carry conviction, but it would be proof of Roper's presence and his reputation would do the rest.

"You fool," said Tharol Sen. "I'm a witness, and I saw you do that. I'll testify."

"Do that," taunted Torry viciously, "if it ever comes to a trial. Who'll believe you? And I don't think the strong-arm boys will wait for a trial. If you can get back through that transmitter screen, we'd better do it before someone finds us here."

"Take you?" she snarled. "I d rather die here."

"You have that choice."

She changed her mind. Torry did not misread the flash of wicked triumph on her face. He did not have to.

"All right," she yielded. "Bart Roper will know how to take care of you. Come ahead, if you dare. The transmitter screen is in the opposite office."

Torry sighed bitterly. "I'll chance Roper. I've already had one session with the goons."

THE quicksilver screen was three-dimensional, and possibly four, since it seemed to exist in two places at once and linked them without regard to intervening distance. It was a hollow cylinder supported by metal framework, and the insubstantial fabric glowed and pulsed with electrical current. Inside was darkness and a sense of infinite space. Walking through the odd fabric one encountered nothing material, but a prickling touched every skin surface, then soaked through the bone centers.

Leaving the force field of the screen was more exhilarating, and almost painful. It was like breaking an electrical contact; muscles jerked spasmodically, hair stood on end, and hot sparks discharged from any moist portions of the skin. Torry had not realized how drenched his body was in cold sweat. He stepped out, gasping.

He stepped into paradise, or hell. Unreality.

Martian subcellar gardens are startling to outsiders. In the air was the bitter tang of narcotic incense. Smoke distorted vision. Nightmarish fantasies of mobile murals in rich colors writhed on the walls. The ceiling was an illusion of sky and stars, complete with intricacies of celestial mechanics, and the flooring resembled grassy sward, set with miniature pools and cool, gurgling streams, crossed by arching bridges of carved and tined ivory. Singing birds and trilling winged serpents filled the air with sound and motion. Luminous bubbles rose and burst above lighted, musical fountains. Musicians toyed with the acrid melodies of ancient Mars, and only close inspection proved the dancing girls to be 3-D projections.

It was a painstaking reproduction, pitiful and exquisite, of the richly barbaric and luxuriant youth of a now-dying planet. To a Martian, it would have been nostalgic and lovely. To Torry, fresh from the scent of blood and death, it was a garish mockery, like a painted corpse.

Torry recoiled painfully, both from the setting and from the living man who seemed part of it.

Sen Bas was as dried and shriveled as a Martian mummy. Only his eyes seemed alive.

"You can put away your gun," said Sen Bas, his wrinkled face a mask of malicious humor. "You are in no danger here."

Oddly, there was no feeling of menace, and Torry found himself putting away his weapon. Will power beat from Sen Bas as it does from hypno machines, and his personality held fearful compulsion.

"But he's—" began Tharol Sen hysterically.

Still smiling, Sen Bas nodded like a bizarre doll with a swinging pendulum attached to its head. "No matter. Since we made a deal with Roper when we picked him up off Phobos, we must do as he says…in some matters. Roper has gone ahead. He wants this man, Torry, sent to him…there. There is use for him…where Roper has gone. Until then, he is our guest, and we must show him every courtesy."

Torry studied the old man calmly. "You can use place names, Sen Bas. I know about the transuranics on Triton and Pluto. But how could Roper have gone ahead when we were using the transmitter? It can't be three places at once."

Sen Bas frowned. "No, it cannot. Unfortunately, it has many limitations. This is a second model copied by my engineers for study and experiment. To our distress we have learned that ores of the heavy metals cannot be transmitted since their radioactivity has an effect on the force field. But now, with trouble coming, this model must be destroyed."

From a pouch Sen Bas drew a tiny subsonic whistle upon which he blew a soundless note. Martian technicians quickly appeared. Sen Bas issued commands, and the transmitter was rapidly dismantled and removed to incinerators.

"Good idea," approved Torry. "Ferax is dead. The police—"

"I know, I know. The transmitter is really not as instantaneous as it seems to the user. Time also is distorted, as well as space. Hours have passed. You are the last person known to have seen Ferax, so you are wanted by the police and others for questioning. I was not certain you would come through the screens, so my agents are scouring the city for you. Roper has gone ahead to Triton, and wants you to join him there where we can make contact."

"How long will that take?"

Sen Bas blinked. "Who knows? My scientists say it depends on the relative positions of Triton and Mars. The best time will be in five or six days, but you may have to go sooner. Tharol Sen can show you around, and when the time is right, she will take you to the transmitter. It is securely hidden where the police will not find it. In the meantime—"

"I'm a prisoner?"

Sen Bas giggled for a moment. "Not exactly. Say, my guest—the only jailers you have are outside. Let us hope they will stay there until you can go to Roper...as he requested."

"Roper must have been in a hurry to get away," grated Torry.

"He was. For excellent reasons. A Solar Survey ship is due off Triton at any time. Roper wanted to be in sole possession of the satellite, with samples to make good his claims to minerals."

Suddenly, everything happened at once. Shrill alarms blared from a dozen quarters. Red lights flared ominously. A fusillade of shots broke out.

Sen Bas swore luridly in Martian. "The police!"

Heavy explosions thundered overhead. The ceiling cracked, opened wide. An avalanche of steel and stone and breaking glass roared into the subcellar gardens. Dust clouds blinded Torry.

CHAPTER FIVE

FROM the collapsing roof tons of debris poured into the underground gardens and spread over the floor like advancing mountains. Dust choked, Torry staggered blindly before it in panic to avoid being caught and buried. It was like a swift, deadly race with an engulfing landslide.

Free of the confusion and deafening tumult, he turned to look about for Sen Bas and the girl. In the dust cloud it was impossible to see anything. Masses of masonry and fused glass from the collapsing cavern roof continued to detach themselves and crash down in random uproar. Cautiously, Torry picked his way over the mounds of rubble, searching.

A feeble cry led him to Sen Bas. The aged Martian looked like a tattered bundle of red rags. Half buried under a hillock of shattered stone and twisted steel, the old man showed little sign of life, save for still-glittering eyes and husks of sound emerging from bloodless lips. Spreading stains of red seeped from beneath the prisoning blocks.

"If I can lift the stones, can you drag yourself out?" asked Torry.

"Don't—think—so!" gasped Sen Bas.

"Where can I find help?"

"Don't try. Go—quickly. Save yourself. The alarms—police—maybe union killers. Go—"

"Not yet," snapped Torry. "We'll worry about the rest after I get you out."

The old man protested. "I'm—old. Does not matter. Get to—transmitter. My people must have—"

Ignoring him, Torry worked. Feverishly he searched for and found a length of reinforcing steel. With it, he dug into debris of glass and stone and tortured steel. Mass by mass, he levered it up and rolled it aside. Fingers raw, steel bending in his hands, he strained to uncover the writhing, bleeding form of Sen Bas. At last he wedged up the last mass and reached under to drag out the ancient Martian. Sen Bas screamed as he came free, but the agony left his face.

"You're hurting him," raged Tharol Sen. She stumbled toward them, her face a mask of hate.

"No!" cried Sen Bas. Gathering breath, he whispered, "He saved me." Then pallor flooded his pinched features.

Torry knelt beside him, not even looking at the girl. "Shut up!" he ordered. "Get bandages—painkilling drugs. He's badly crushed, bleeding to death. Don't argue. Hurry!"

Sen Bas blinked. "Do as he says..." Tharol Sen disappeared.

Alone, Sen Bas stared curiously at his rescuer. "I should have ordered you both to the transmitter. My men could care for me...if it matters."

"Not soon enough. Roper can wait."

Sen Bas shook his head. "Roper might. My people cannot. We need heavier metals to power our underground cities. We are a dying race."

"You're a dying man. Don't talk."

The old Martian composed his features with great dignity. "What better time? Our need is desperate. We must claim the transuranics on Triton. Even though they must be freighted here, since they cannot be brought through the transmitter. We tried it, and failed. You know Roper. Will he deal fairly with us?"

Torry shook his head sadly. "No."

Sen Bas did not seem surprised. "I feared that. Will you?"

"I'll try, though I'll have to do what seems best when I get to it."

Sen Bas relaxed. "That is good enough. Did you come to Mars to kill him?"

A shiver wrenched Torry, his eyes glazed. "I haven't decided yet."

"Perhaps it would be best. But he will not be easy to kill. Tharol Sen will take you to him. Perhaps by the time fate has to choose between you and Roper, her blindness will be gone, and she can make a clear choice of her own..."

"How did you—"

With a convulsive grimace, Sen Bas was dead. Moments later, when Tharol Sen appeared loaded with medical supplies, Torry glared at her. Her face a chalk mask, she whimpered.

"Forget it," Torry said angrily. "It's too late for tears."

"Why did you try to save him?"

"If you have to ask, you'd never understand."

Tharol Sen shuddered. "I don't understand anything about you. Who you are. Why you hate us so—"

"Who says I do?"

"Roper. He says—"

"Never mind what he says. I suppose there's no use trying to convince you that he never tells the truth if a lie will serve as well. He's a known criminal, a thief and swindler, and even a murderer. A man who abandoned his wife on Earth, and has a small child he's never seen.

Frankly, I don't understand you, and I'm not sure I'd want to. You're quite determined to marry him?"

"Quite." Tharol Sen stiffened.

"Well, that's your hard luck. He's no good. No good for you, or anyone. Not even for himself."

"Nothing you can say matters. He told me about that wife. She's too sane, too normal and practical for him. He thinks that I—"

Torry was not listening. Contrasting Tharol Sen with Rose, he was almost inclined to agree with Roper, and envy him such a loyal and spirited defender. The girl was pure blood Martian, with all the eerie beauty of the strange race. She was young and vibrantly alive and human. There was emotional depth in her, and a passionate savagery that might inspire a man to passion, or to devotion, depending upon the man.

"Besides," finished Tharol Sen, "there is no other man like him."

"Not quite like him, fortunately," Torry laughed bitterly. "I'm a lot like him, if you haven't noticed. But nicer...and sometimes smarter."

"That's a matter of opinion," she said acidly. "Yours and mine. But you do resemble him. You're...you're not—"

"I'm afraid I am. I'm ashamed to admit it, but Bart Roper and I had the same mother. He's my half-brother."

HER face was puzzled. "Then why—"

Torry tightened visibly. "I don't know. Or maybe I just don't want to face it yet. We hate each other as only brothers can. You'd better know that before you take me to him. I may have to kill him."

Tharol Sen sneered. "I don't think you can kill him. I'll take you to him because both Roper and my grandfather wanted me to. Roper can deal with you as he sees fit. But if I think you're a danger to him, I'll kill you. Understand that."

Torry shrugged. "On that basis I'll accept your help. Now you'd better find that transmitter. I suspect that the explosions were the police or the goon squads breaking in."

"They were," she said nastily. "They ran into booby traps in the upper levels. It will take them a while."

"I wouldn't count on too much time," warned Torry. "Grannar is a smart policeman, and the goon squads seemed to know their work."

"This way."

Tharol Sen was coldly aloof, and seemed both preoccupied and depressed, which was natural. She went ahead, wordlessly, and Torry followed, lost in his own reflections. At the far end of Sen Bas' wrecked garden was a steel-arched doorway, high, sombre, and gothic. Beyond, and below, lay the sprawling vastness of vaults and caverns that was the Martian underworld. Long, curving ramps led downward into a complex of subsurface workings far below New Chicago.

They descended and slipped quietly across large, echoing platforms whose dimensions were lost in gloom. Metal-shod stairways spiraled upward and downward into invisible infinities. Deep shafts vibrated with strange sounds the ear could not catch or identify. Freight tunnels were yawning maws of darkness, like the staring, sightless eyes of some mythical monster created on too large a scale for man to understand.

Torry grew tense and nervous. He began to sense patterns of shivering, eerie movement about him. Walls and ceilings closed in suddenly, and he could make out vague, monstrous forms set into niches within walls carved of bedrock—old Martian gods in sculpture-leering stone spectres, goblin-like, and subtly obscene.

Tharol Sen paused. Her hand sought Torry's and drew him close, but not in friendliness. She whispered harshly, warning him to silence and extreme caution.

"I was wrong. The police have broken through. Some are already in the vaults."

She followed a maze of barely visible threadlike guidelines of luminosity set into the metallic tiling. A few steps more brought them to a wide platform, from which many tunnel mouths opened. Along one wall ranged banks of elevators. Beyond were ranks of empty pneumatic tube cars on tracks that angled in sharp descent into wells a level below the platform. Spidery Martian hieroglyphs labeled various shafts and the tube terminals. Tharol Sen studied the markings closely before making her choice.

"I have been here only once before," she complained. "It is not easy to find the way. But I think the police will have more trouble."

She selected a pneumatic tube car. Torry boosted her to the door flap. She settled herself in the tiny seat cradle, then from inside, extended him a helping hand. For the first time she noticed his blistered palms and raw fingers. He grunted painfully as she drew him up beside her.

"I should have bandaged your hands," she mused.

Torry snorted, "Can you drive this shuttle? It has more gadgets than a space ship."

"One way to find out," murmured Tharol Sen icily, poking a slim finger at a keyboard of colored studs.

Distant machinery whirred and whined. Flaps banged shut and the shuttle car shot forward and down at sickening speed. Tharol Sen laughed, and the sound was of ice chips trickling on metal foil.

Air whipped angrily about the shell of thin metal. There was no gut wrenching nausea of acceleration, only sharp awareness of speed. Movement became a blur streaming past the transparent plastic cartop. It was like being part of a hollow missile fired from an air gun. As the car's original impetus diminished, speed dwindled. The car dipped and slowed, then ran into a stop valve, like a piston in a closed cylinder, and stopped on a dense cushion of compressed air.

Another vista of platforms radiated away from the terminal.

Gripping Torry's hand, Tharol Sen dragged him firmly along the platform, then down a steep slant to the lowest levels. At intervals, radilumes provided glaring light, but shadows of raw fantasy lingered curiously near the walls. Tomblike oppression gathered around them. Panic grows quickly underground; weight of rock pressing overhead translates itself to the brain in terms of claustrophobia.

METALLIC decking became raw stone floor, and an endless tunnel unwound before them. Torry lost all track of direction, even the primary up and down. They went through underground workings like city streets lined with open front factories. Gray, barren vistas of workrooms were relieved by the stark symmetries of sleek machines, shielded atomic converters, and patiently revolving turbines. Here was the marvelously efficient underground economy of the old Martian civilization, still functioning and serving the remnants of a great, race of builders and scientists.

On soaring cantilevered balconies and in alcoves, Torry glimpsed cliff like structures of offices and dwellings. Giant compressors labored to force a mighty pulse of breakable air—but the atmosphere was warm, dry and stifling. Runnels of sweat ran down Torry's body and vanished in quick evaporation; fever and exertion alternated in him; he blew hot and cold as energy burned away too quickly, and as drying sweat produced intense, quick chills. Temperatures dropped. Air seemed denser and was poisonously clouded with dust, but it was cool. Slowly it became chill and depressing with a hint of dampness in it. They came into a maze of galleries and pits, tunnels and vaults, less used and uninhabited portions of the deep-workings.

It was like a world apart, a place of dim storage bins with natural refrigeration, of packing sheds piled high with mountains of commercial molds, bales of dry, compressed and packed mushrooms. It smelled stale and foul, the air hideous with a powdery mist of mold dust and spores, and the incredible mustiness of mushroom spoilage. These caverns were empty of life, as if the troglodyte Martians had long ago joined their mummied dead.

Weakness suddenly caught up with Torry. Dizzy, he reached in panic at Tharol Sen for support. Grudgingly, after a moment's hesitation, she granted the help.

"I'm sorry," Torry apologized. "It's been a rather active three days. I guess Ferax and his boys hurt me more than I had thought."

"They are good at hurting people," admitted the girl. "You still want to go on in this condition?"

"Don't mind me. Just give me a minute," Torry was painfully aware of her strong, slender body beneath the filmy garments of spidersilk. To change the subject, he said, "Don't tell me you're planning to venture out to Pluto or Triton in that costume?"

Tharol Sen made a face. "Hardly. There are spacesuits ready. We'll need them, don't worry. Roper says Triton is hardly livable at all, even protected. You'll find out if you've the nerve to go through with me."

"So Planet X is not even a planet, just one of Neptune's moons?"

"Perhaps it was a planet once. Both Pluto and Triton are not like the rest of the solar system planets. They may have been two stray worlds from outer space, captured long ago by our sun. For their size they have mass out of all proportion. The quantities of heavy metals beyond uranium give them extreme weight and density. Pluto has a density of over fifty times that of water. Triton not so much, but still greater by far than Earth's density, which is roughly five or six times that of water. Though smaller than Mercury or Ganymede, Triton has a gravity only slightly less than Earth's and a far denser atmosphere blanket."

Torry laughed grimly. "That's a big speech for you."

"Too long a speech," she agreed irritably. "Especially with the police close behind us."

Torry sighed. "Okay. We'll go on. This is a lot of trouble over one slimy mirage salesman."

"Mirage salesman? Why do you call him that?"

"Simple enough. That's all he's ever peddled. Pot of gold at the end of the rainbow to tempt the greedy and unwary. And rainbows are circular, with no beginning and no end. Haven't you ever heard the term?"

"I have now. I wondered. That's all. There are mirages on Triton. He'll have plenty to sell."

Torry snorted. "I can see you've bought one."

Flasher signals on the wall began to blink rapidly.

They moved steadily onward, faster than before, into a still more shadowy region. Light itself seemed to exist only at long intervals where age-old radilumes performed a feeble service. The spongy floor of rotten bedrock was scummed over with moss to make for slippery footing. Formations of natural rock seemed like stage furniture designed by elves and gnomes, in which stone mimicked monstrosities of the vegetable world. Fat, knotted stalagmites suggested tree trunks, and the darkness overhead appeared like shadowy densities of foliage. Seepage had fretted the walls into lacy limestone traceries like a fern forest. They went on, with tense silence savage between them.

Alarm blinkers flashed light codes of rapid pursuit.

"Your people must have had much contact with the police to have worked out such a set-up," observed Torry.

Tharol Sen nodded. "We have been persecuted for centuries. Not many Earthfolk have ever been here. Nor any others but my own people."

"Yet the police seem to be finding their way."

Tharol Sen frowned. "That puzzles me," she admitted. "How could they come here at all unless someone has betrayed us?"

From close behind sounded the loud buzzing of a radiation detector. A thin pencil beam flashed at them and splashed wetly over the cavern wall ahead. Rock shattered in a brittle, crunchy explosion. Murderous chips deluged the tunnel.

Torry lunged at the girl, dragging her down in a savage fall. More beams of light licked out, this time from several directions. Continuous thunders roared and reverberated, stunning ears and brains with concussion and sound. Roughly, Torry thrust the girl into a wall niche for shelter.

"The police!" wailed Tharol Sen.

"Looks as if we're trapped. We'd better give ourselves up."

She stared at him with contempt. "You still have your gun. If you're afraid, give it to me."

"One gun against a dozen. No thanks."

Waiting a lull in the blast uproar, Torry called out. His voice rang hollowly in the cavern, still shuddering with echoes of the explosions.

"Hold your fire. We're coming out."

Grannar's voice answered. "Throw out your gun first."

Torry complied. His gun rattled on the floor of rock.

Pushing Tharol Sen sullenly before him, Torry stood clear. In a moment, the tunnel was full of uniformed figures.

Grannar studied Torry with some amusement. "You needn't have gone so fast. I got your note, but your trail ran into a dead end at Ferax's office. It took time to pick it up again but we found it beside Sen Bas' body in his gardens. Clever deal, Torry. Using radioactive dust on your shoes like that. Shall we handcuff Tharol Sen and take her back?"

"No," answered Torry glumly. "She's going to show us the way to Roper."

"So you betrayed us?" asked Tharol Sen, contempt making her face ugly.

"That's a matter of opinion."

Grannar broke in. "Better pick up your gun, Torry. You may need it. How many men shall we take?"

Torry shrugged. "That depends on the number of spacesuits available. How many, Tharol Sen?"

"Three," she replied bitterly. "Do you think two of you dare tackle Roper alone?"

"I think so. How about it, Grannar?"

The policeman grunted.

The matter transmitter was already set up. Upon its folding framework the screen glittered like woven quicksilver, vibrating to the hum of electro magnetic flow.

"Will this take us directly to Roper?" asked Grannar.

"Not quite," said Torry, grinning. "It's a delicate adjustment. Mars and Neptune both in motion, and Triton's orbit and axial rotation to consider. We'll be somewhere on Triton—"

"But Triton has more land surface than Earth. Can we find—"

Torry gestured. "She'll find him for us. Have your men stand by and switch on the transmitter every three hours."

Dressed for space, the three entered the screen.

CHAPTER SIX

PLANET X—or Neptune's moon, Triton—was a vast mirage with many facets. Atmosphere was as dense and still as water in ocean deeps. Sky was cloudless, but not clear, apparently built up of different layers of gases, and the light was both glazing and erratic. At a distance of over three and a half billion miles from the Sun, most of the light was not sunlight, and the little that came through the air ocean was filtered and absorbed into curious colors and intensities. Other illumination sources were auroral displays, radioactive hotspots that glowed like eerie ghosts, and volcanic outbursts of crimson or gold.

Surface pressure of the atmospheric ocean was extreme, and the gas densities and weird light gave an uncanny submarine illusion. Venturing onto the surface of Triton, Torry felt like a diver in that long-past period when man's last frontier on Earth had seemed the ocean deeps. Gravity, greater than on Mars, but less than Earth's, gave a sense of buoyancy; the spacesuiting was not unlike ancient diving costume; and the thickness of the atmosphere itself suggested deep, still water.

Most disturbing of all were the mirages. All the familiar effects of Earth mirages were present but magnified and even multiplied into infinite complexities. To a scientist of optics or meteorology, Triton would be a superb laboratory. To Torry, it was—

Near madness...!

Mirages by hundreds and thousands floated between surface and zenith, or hugged the ground like captive nightmares. Pinnacled dream mountains rose from bases of empty air. Phantom battlements and mock castles stormed upward from nothing. Magnified rockeries became goblin cities, looming near or far in equal scale. Water glittered in the sky and on the ground, and floating debris became fleets of fairy argosies. Lateral mirages played eerie jokes with distance. All images seemed unreal, and diffraction haloed them with misty, rainbow coloring.

Triton itself was bleak, savage, merciless, nearly windless but for vagrant currents of slow-moving dense air, like currents in an ocean.

By levels, temperatures were absurdly high or low, depending upon location or freak circumstances. It was a lifeless world, inhospitable to man. But it wore a mask and costume of exotic, lying beauty, and masquerade was hard to distinguish from the harsh reality. Anything definite was hard to distinguish.

Grannar turned up the microphone in his helmet, and his words rattled from Torry's speaker.

"How can we find Roper in such a madhouse as this?" he roared.

Torry winced as the amplified outburst thundered in his ears.

"Simple enough," he replied. "Fine detective you are. There's a radio compass built into Tharol Sen's suit. Roper's sending all the time. She'll go to him like a homing pigeon."

"Pigeon is right," muttered Grannar. "Hope it's not too far. A little more of this would make me neurotic. Can we trust her?"

Torry laughed. "Yes and no. She hates us, but she'll lead us to Roper. The matter transmitter is his only way back to Mars. And hers, too. Isn't that right, Tharol Sen?"

Fortunately her reply did not come through clearly.

Following the radio compass, which behaved erratically due to magnetic discharges, they moved through the wilderness of the mirages. Progress was deceptive, without reliable landmarks. Rugged terrain made treacherous going. Megalithic cities and monstrous mountains appeared and disappeared like patterns in a kaleidoscope. In the eccentric lighting, vision itself seemed to flicker as treacherously as a 3-D projector running out of balance. Constant distortions and fading out produced mental nausea and physical insecurity.

Torry was not sure where his next step would take him. One instant he seemed to flounder on the edge of abyss. The next, he would be climbing what seemed an interminable mountain, only to have solid floors of rock shimmer and vanish before his eyes. It was impossible to see where they were going, or even be certain what it was like where they had just been. Only the needle of the radio compass held any steadiness at all, and that jerked into wild whirlings now and then as magnetic currents ebbed and flowed in the ground.

They seemed, through rifts in the mirages, to be traversing a monstrous field of jagged boulders, inclined slightly upward. Even these rocks were not always as substantial as they looked, but for the most part, they were real obstacles. The thought crossed Torry's mind that it would be a bad place for an ambush if Roper were so inclined.

When the facts materialized his fears, the pencil beam of a blaster cutting through the mirages seemed only part of a dazzling auroral display.

THE explosion that followed demonstrated its reality. Rock chips and larger fragments rained about them. In the dense medium of atmosphere, the shock wave was terrific, and even his spacesuit did not completely insulate the blow. All three were flung about as if by earthquake. Torry missed his footing and went down in a long sprawl, which actually saved his life.

The second blaster flash would have targeted him dead center. It flickered harmless over him and torched the nearby boulders to a sudden glare, then lost itself in fearful detonation. Dodging the hail of debris, Torry crawled quickly to shelter behind a larger boulder. With gauntleted hands, he tested its solidity before he trusted himself to relax.

A harsh cry of pain and terror echoed in his ears. Its tones held desperation. And the voice was Grannar's.

By concentrating Torry could dimly make out the figure of the detective. Grannar lay in tumbled heap, threshing wildly and trying to hold shut great rents in his space suit and helmet. He seemed to be injured, for one leg was motionless while the rest of his body worked in convulsions.

Torry left his shelter and bounded toward the casualty. He bundled Grannar roughly to his feet and hustled him into the nearest tangle of solid rocks. A hastily aimed blaster beam hurried him at the task. Crouching down, he examined Grannar. The policeman was conscious, swearing valiantly. His leg was broken. Inside the space suit it would be impossible to set the fracture. And outside, the toxic gases of Triton would make short work of human breathing. Even the rents in the suiting and the cracks in his helmet were dangerous.

Working quickly, Torry clipped together the rents and sealed them hermetically with compound from the repair kits. He did the same for the helmet cracks.

"That's the best I can do," he told the policeman grimly as his eyes searched in vain for a sign of Roper. "You'll have to stand the pain till we can get out of here and back to Mars."

"'What are our chances of getting out?"

A man does not shrug in a spacesuit. "Not good," said Torry. "Roper can keep us pinned here as long as he likes."

"How long d'you think that'll be?"

Torry grunted. "Till he gets tired of it and decides to stalk us and kill us. Or till I go out and get him."

"I see. It's like that, eh? Where's the girl?"

"Who knows? She's either hiding out in the rocks, like us, or she's found a way to join Roper. Does it matter?"

"Not to me," mused Grannar. "I just hoped maybe she wasn't as rotten as Roper...that she might give us a chance."

"Don't count on it," said Torry spitefully. "She might be as pure as an angel, but Roper's sold her a bill of goods. Feeling as she does about him, she'd kill either of us as quickly as Roper would."

They waited in silence while mirages came and went around them, as light shifted, or slight currents stirred in the turbid air. If Roper were a mirage salesman, he had certainly made his stand in the wholesale house. Under other circumstances, Torry might have found the displays interesting, even entertaining—but at the moment, his reflections were as poisonous as the air on Triton.

Colors flared and faded like a cross-spectrum of inferno.

Grannar was restless with the pain in his leg. His squirming infected Torry, who leaned out above the barrier of rocks waving his hand violently. As he hoped, he attracted attention. A thin wire of light kissed the rocks of the barrier. Chips pelted like hail, and the force of the blast set up thunderous echoes in his helmet.

"He must have rigged a scanner of some sort. Such shooting is too good for a man with mirages in his eyes. Would something like infra-red help?"

"I don't know," groaned Grannar. "In any case, we haven't the time or the means to work out a scanner."

"I think I'll try crawling out of here. If I keep low, I might be able to work around and come up behind him. Is it all right with you if I give it a try?"

"Why not? Outside of your life, what have you got to lose?"

"I hate to leave you here unless you want it that way. But there's not much future for you, anyhow, if I stay."

"Do whatever you like. I guess I owe you something, and I like to pay my debts. Any other last wishes?"

"Just one. I want him…"

"Roper? You want to kill him?" Grannar sounded baffled.

"Kill or cure."

"I don't understand."

"You want him on Mars for murder. He's wanted on Earth for lesser crimes. That gives you priority. You can demand and get extradition for him to Mars, which means quick death in the atomic disintegrators, or slow death in the prison mines. On Earth, they have a clinic for incurables like Roper. It's a free choice for them, euthanasia or voluntary submission to the clinic."

Grannar hesitated. "I know about that. But isn't such a treatment almost as dangerous as being killed outright, and a lot tougher on the subject?"

"It can be," granted Torry flatly. "Sometimes the hypnotic memory-blanking or the shock treatment wrecks the brain. And the glandular surgery and hormone dosage can turn a man into a freak and monster. If it works, the criminal is rebuilt mentally and morally, re-created with a new personality, and completely new educational background. He's hardly the same man, and often his old friends can't recognize him physically."

Grannar's eyes narrowed. "In Roper's case, that might be an advantage. Of course I'm familiar with the clinic and its work in rehabilitating incorrigibles, but do you think any treatment could work the miracle with Roper?"

"I don't know and don't care. People like Roper help make life colorful and interesting. But they're too hard on everyone around them. His adolescent-stasis carries his own damnation for him. He's miserably unhappy, along with everyone who knows him. He imagines he's smarter and superior to other people, and that it's his duty to prey on them. Mentally, he's a rotten spoiled child. But a dangerous one. Like the one rotten apple, he spreads his rottenness through the whole barrel."

"I'm familiar with that theory of crime but I don't go along with it. I'm not convinced you can unspoil a rotten apple, and I doubt if it's worthwhile to try."

"No matter," said Torry grimly. "If they fail on him, they'll destroy him. Either way, it will make a better world for everyone. Probably I hate him more than you do. But I'm willing to give him this last chance if you'll let me."

Grannar laughed ironically. "Have it your way, if you can take him. It's out of my hands, actually. Though, as a cop, I'd be better satisfied if you burned him down here. I'll settle for your clinic. It's a nasty enough choice, anyhow. If you can capture or kill him, go ahead. I'll gladly resign my share of the brute to you. And you'll earn it. Do you really think you can crawl out of here and circle him?"

Torry glanced sourly at the flickering mirages. "I can try," he said slowly.

CHAPTER SEVEN

IT WAS a mirage that saved Torry. Crawling out proved even rougher than he had expected. Squirming over unknown terrain is hard, even in conditions of fair visibility. On Triton, with its constantly varying light, and the ever-present confusion of mirages, it was fantastic. The cumbersome spacesuit was no help.

Darkness thickened around him, but the mirages grew worse, as he toiled up the slope. Loose stones rattled about him in tiny avalanches, so he went more carefully, lest they betray him to Roper. Sweat bathed him inside his insulated costume, and steam misted the helmet's faceplate before he could get the thermal conditioners functioning properly. A bad foothold earned him a nasty fall, and the rough suiting and acid sweat combined to burn painful blisters on hands and knees.

In grim determination approximating madness, he plunged upward and onward. He found an eroded ravine and groped blindly along it, wondering what fearful liquids had gashed such a gully on such a nightmarish world.

Alien dusk gathered, and in the hollow of the ravine writhed coils of living light. At intervals, he avoided the hot glaring flares of radioactive hotspots. Torry followed the barren fissure, and strange sounds and fleeting light-phantoms followed him. And a river of dense, sluggish air funneled upward through the gully, whispering of ugly, forgotten events upon a forgotten world. In the uneasy sky overhead, electrical discharges wove networks of colored lightnings, which crackled and hissed as static in his earphones.

Nearing the upper end of the gully, Torry halted and took stock of his surroundings. He estimated progress, and wondered how he would ever find his quarry. His quest seemed one more mad illusion in the sequence of mirages. He freed his blaster from its magnetic belt clip and examined it for charge. Crawling with the weapon in his hand was awkward, but it would be suicide to be caught reaching for it. Grimly he worked his way to the notch of the ravine and poked out his head.

Ironically, it was the mirage that saved him.

A lateral mirage, distorting both distance and direction, showed him a sharp image, inverted, of Roper aiming carefully in the opposite direction.

Instantly, Torry let go his grasp and dropped. He fell and rolled savagely, while the lance of light stabbed overhead, and the explosion started small landslides around him. He screamed in momentary panic. Preventing a helpless plunge into an abyss that opened before him was a chore. And the abyss itself proved only illusion. Solid wall blocked his fall and stunned him for a terrible moment. Miraculously, he retained a grip on his gun.

He lay quietly, while rocks continued to rattle upon his helmet and spacesuit. Someone was descending toward him. It could be only—

Roper.

The visible face behind the plate of transparent plastic could have been poured in the same mold as Torry's. It was younger, finer-featured, but it was shrewd, self-indulgent. Roper had enjoyed his life of crime, and it had agreed with him. He looked healthy, humorously handsome and extremely well fed.

He stared at Torry, and the expression on his face changed as he saw the blaster. He started a movement toward his own clipped weapon.

"Don't try it, Bart," ordered Torry sharply. "I think I'd enjoy killing you."

Bart Roper sighed deeply. "You took unfair advantage of me," he complained. "I thought you were hurt or killed. I was coming to see—"

"To make sure of me, if you'd missed? Maybe not. Maybe you did have a human impulse for once. I'll try to think so. And you can see how much it hurts when someone takes advantage of any human weakness. It hurts, doesn't it?"

Roper nodded slowly. "It does. So you've got me... Don't be so proud of yourself. It wasn't that hard. I was cooked from the moment your police pals got their hands on the transmitter. It was my only way out. You know that, of course. I just wanted the pleasure of taking some of you with me. I'm not going back to Mars. The disintegrators or life in the prison mines don't appeal to me. So you'd better kill me now."

"I will if you force me," Torry told him wearily. "But I'm not making it that easy for you. There's a choice, but you won't like it. I've made a deal with Grannar. You can die now, or you can go back to Earth to the clinic."

"The clinic!" shrieked Roper. "You know what that means, I wouldn't be the same person. Maybe not even human."

Torry steadied his eyes on his brother. "I'm not sure you ever were human. But you need treatment. They'll knock out your thymus, drug you and shock you and carve you till you'll never know yourself. You won't be an antisocial monster with the emotional stasis of a child.

You won't be anything you've ever been. But you may be a man. And you'll stop hurting people, or they'll stop you for good. The choice is yours—right now. So make up both our minds before I decide to shoot."

Roper yielded with a grimace of distaste. "You win, Torry. You always did, sooner or later. I was quicker, but you were smarter. I guess Rose was the last of your toys I'll ever swipe. And it's back to kindergarten for Bart Roper."

Torry relaxed, though he still did not lower his gun.

"You'll be going back on the survey ship, Bart. That way, you'll have a long voyage in the brig to meditate on your sins. But on Earth, you'll have Rose. You're a married man there, with a wife and child. Rose still loves you, Bart. When you steal something, it stays stolen. I'm not going back, so you'll get Rose after all."

Roper laughed coldly. "That's what I meant about your being smarter than I am. You always come out ahead."

Torry's eyes followed a moving mirage to a notch high on the walls of the gully. The glitter of cold metal was not illusion. Tharol Sen held a gun on him, unwaveringly.

"You can come out now," Torry said to her. "It's all over."

Tharol Sen lowered her gun and walked unsteadily toward them.

"Why didn't you shoot?" Roper stormed at her angrily. "You could have killed him before he pulled the trigger."

Inside her faceplate. Torry could see her eyes dim with hot tears.

"Yes, I could have," she said brokenly. "But maybe I've seen enough mirages to recognize one…"

MANY Martian hours later, three people watched the survey ship blast off from Triton. Before the ship left, Grannar had been taken aboard and removed from his spacesuit long enough for drugs to be administered and his legs set and splinted. Now, with painkilling narcotics deadening him, the policeman was scarcely aware of the departing ship with his prisoner aboard, consigned bodily to Earth and its clinic for incurable criminals. Grannar had relaxed into a dope-daydream of a comfortable future on Earth as a plankton farmer, with nothing to do but read minifilm detective stories.

Watching the ship vanish beyond a sky full of mirages, Torry tried vainly to conquer a growing feeling of depression. Loneliness began to sweep over him, as if with the sudden termination of his obsession about Roper, his life had lost most of its meaning. It occurred to him suddenly that Tharol Sen was probably feeling infinitely worse. With a quick glance toward Grannar to make sure that the policeman was all right, Torry climbed slowly to the eyrie in the high rocks where the girl had hidden herself. Like a doll in a space suit, Tharol Sen huddled together, staring upward as if toward some vanishing illusion.

Shared loneliness sometimes loses its sting.

But Tharol Sen ignored Torry's presence, and he felt acutely embarrassed.

"You'll be better off without him," Torry said, consoling her. "And life will be much simpler."

"I know that," she replied sharply. "What else did you want?"

Torry laughed.

"Business, I guess. According to Solar Space Law, we three are the sole owners of the moon Triton and its mineral rights, since we were actually on the spot and in possession when the survey ship arrived. Your people will have the transuranics they need—plenty of it. But the stuff won't work in the transmitter, so it'll have to go in the hard way. High freight charges will cut down the profits, so I really don't think any of us are going to get rich. I'm fairly certain that Grannar will sell his rights for a very cheap price. And as far as I'm concerned, I'd rather your people had the stuff at cost, so I'll sign over my rights to them for the forty-one thousand credits I've already got invested. Also, you can claim complete salvage rights on the transmitter of a third of the value, and I'm sure the inventor will be happy to have it back at that. I won't ask any part of the salvage claim. Money just weighs me down anyhow."

"That's very generous of you—very generous indeed." murmured Tharol Sen. "My people will be very grateful to you."

"And you," he asked. "Just how grateful will you be?"

Her eyes blinked, then stared soberly through the faceplate of her helmet. "Ask that again—"

"It's not part of the deal, of course. But you bragged that you could make Roper forget a girl back on Earth. I need some full time forgetting, and I wondered if you'd like to try the same stunt for me."

Tharol Sen studied him for a long moment before answering.

"When we're out of these helmets," she said softly, "you can kiss me. Just once. For gratitude. Afterward, much later, we can think about the rest, and discuss it with dignity. If you're staying on Mars, why not look me up...sometime?"

"Why not?" asked Torry, grinning. Then without waiting for the kiss, he made his decision. "And I'm staying on Mars..."

THE END

If you've enjoyed this book, you will not want to miss these terrific titles…

ARMCHAIR MYSTERY & SCIENCE FICTION CLASSICS
$12.95 each

C-40 **MODEL FOR MURDER**
by Stephen Marlowe

C-41 **PRELUDE TO MURDER**
by Sterling Noel

C-42 **DEAD WEIGHT**
by Frank Kane

C-43 **A DAME CALLED MURDER**
by Milton Ozaki

C-44 **THE GREATEST ADVENTURE**
by John Taine

C-45 **THE EXILE OF TIME**
by Ray Cummings

C-46 **STORM OVER WARLOCK**
by Andre Norton

C-47 **MAN OF MANY MINDS**
by E. Everett Evans

C-48 **THE GODS OF MARS**
by Edgar Rice Burroughs

C-49 **BRIGANDS OF THE MOON**
by Ray Cummings

C-50 **SPACE HOUNDS OF IPC**
by E. E. "Doc" Smith

C-51 **THE LANI PEOPLE**
by J. F. Bone

C-52 **THE MOON POOL**
by A. Merritt

C-53 **IN THE DAYS OF THE COMET**
by H. G. Wells

C-54 **TRIPLANETARY**
E. E. Doc Smith

If you've enjoyed this book, you will not want to miss these terrific titles...

ARMCHAIR SCI-FI & HORROR DOUBLE NOVELS, $12.95 each

D-121 **THE GENIUS BEASTS** by Frederik Pohl
THIS WORLD IS TABOO by Murray Leinster

D-122 **THE COSMIC LOOTERS** by Edmond Hamilton
WANDL THE INVADER by Ray Cummings

D-123 **ROBOT MEN OF BUBBLE CITY** by Rog Phillips
DRAGON ARMY by William Morrison

D-124 **LAND BEYOND THE LENS** by S. J. Byrne
DIPLOMAT-AT-ARMS by Keith Laumer

D-125 **VOYAGE OF THE ASTEROID, THE** by Laurence Manning
REVOLT OF THE OUTWORLDS by Milton Lesser

D-126 **OUTLAW IN THE SKY** by Chester S. Geier
LEGACY FROM MARS by Raymond Z. Gallun

D-127 **THE GREAT FLYING SAUCER INVASION** by Geoff St. Reynard
THE BIG TIME by Fritz Leiber

D-128 **MIRAGE FOR PLANET X** by Stanley Mullen
POLICE YOUR PLANET by Lester del Rey

D-129 **THE BRAIN SINNERS** by Alan E. Nourse
DEATH FROM THE SKIES by A. Hyatt Verrill

D-139 **CRY CHAOS** by Dwight V. Swain
THE DOOR THROUGH SPACE By Marion Zimmer Bradley

ARMCHAIR SCIENCE FICTION CLASSICS, $12.95 each

C-55 **UNDER THE TRIPLE SUNS**
by Stanton A. Coblentz

C-56 **STONE FROM THE GREEN STAR**
by Jack Williamson

C-57 **ALIEN MINDS**
by E. Everett Evans

ARMCHAIR MASTERS OF SCIENCE FICTION SERIES, $16.95 each

G-13 **SCIENCE FICTION GEMS, Vol. Seven**
Jack Vance and others

G-14 **HORROR GEMS, Vol. Seven**
Robert Bloch and others

HIS TICKET TO MARS WAS STAMPED: "ONE-WAY"

Lester Del Rey's "Police Your Planet" is a good old-fashioned science fiction adventure yarn. Yet it also has all the earmarks of a gritty hard-boiled cop novel. It's the story of Bruce Gordon, a man sent to Mars with a one-way ticket. A man with a controversial past who faces danger and corruption in the far-off city of Marsport, Gordon wasn't crazy about the town, which was basically a central city covered by gigantic air dome surrounded by a massive slum. Gordon soon found himself tangled in a web of intrigue, caught in the middle between two warring factions, both riddled in corruption. He is soon attacked with fists, knives, clubs, and guns (nope, not ray-guns—these things fire bullets!) But the key for Bruce Gordon was finding a way to bring both sides to their knees without losing his life!

ABOUT LESTER DEL REY

Lester del Ray was born Leonard Knapp, in Saratoga, Minnesota, June 2, 1915. Del Rey often told people that his real name was Ramon Felipe Alvarez-del Rey. He also claimed that his family was killed in a car accident in 1935. However, his sister later confirmed that his name was really Leonard Knapp and that the accident in 1935 killed his first wife but not his parents, brother, or sister. Del Rey gained fame as a noted American science fiction author and editor. In his career, he wrote over a hundred short stories and over two dozen novels, including the highly touted "Nerves" in 1956. He was the editor of such magazines as *Space Science Fiction*, *Science Fiction Adventures*, *Rocket Stories*, and a most successful line of Ballantine "del Rey" paperbacks starting in 1977. Some known pen names used by del Rey were John Alvarez, Marion Henry, Philip James, Philip St. John, Charles Satterfield, and Erik van Lihn. In the 1950s, del Rey was one of the main authors writing science fiction for adolescents (along with Robert Heinlein and Andre Norton). Lester del Rey passed away in New York City, on May 10th, 1993. He was 77 years old.

POLICE YOUR PLANET

By
LESTER DEL REY

ARMCHAIR FICTION
PO Box 4369, Medford, Oregon 97501-0168

CHAPTER ONE
One Way Ticket

There were ten passengers in the little pressurized cabin of the electric bus that shuttled between the rocket field and Marsport. Ten men, the driver—and Bruce Gordon.

He sat apart from the others, as he had kept to himself on the ten-day trip between Earth and Mars, with the yellow stub of his ticket still stuck defiantly in the band of his hat, proclaiming that Earth had paid his passage without his permission being asked. His big, lean body was slumped slightly in the seat. There was no expression on his face.

He listened to the driver explaining to a couple of firsters that they were actually on what appeared to be one of the mysterious canals when viewed from Earth. Every book on Mars gave the fact that the canals were either an illusion or something which could not be detected on the surface of the planet.

He glanced back toward the rocket that still pointed skyward back on the field, and then forward toward the city of Marsport, sprawling out in a mess of slums beyond the edges of the dome that had been built to hold air over the central part. And at last he stirred and reached for the yellow stub.

He grimaced at the One Way stamped on it, then tore it into bits and let the pieces scatter over the floor. He counted them as they fell; thirty pieces, one for each year of his life. Little ones for the two years he'd wasted as a cop. Shreds for the four years as a kid in the ring before that—he'd never made the top. Bigger bits for two years also wasted in trying his hand at professional gambling; and the six final pieces that spelled his rise from a special reporter helping out with a police shake-up coverage, through a regular leg-man turning up rackets, and on up like a meteor until… He'd made his big scoop, all right. He'd dug up enough about the Mercury scandals to double circulation.

And the government had explained what a fool he'd been for printing half of a story that was never supposed to be printed until all could be revealed. They'd given Bruce Gordon his final assignment.

He shrugged. He'd bought a suit of airtight coveralls and a helmet at the field; he had some cash, and a set of reader cards in his pocket. The supply house, Earthside, had assured him that this pattern had never been exported to Mars. With them and the knife he'd selected, he might get by.

The Solar Security office had given him the knife practice, to make sure he could use it, just as they'd made sure he hadn't taken extra money with him beyond the regulation amount.

"You're a traitor, and we'd like nothing better than seeing your guts spilled," the Security man had told him. "That paper you swiped was marked top secret. But we don't get many men with your background—cop, tinhorn, fighter—who have brains enough for our work. So you're bound for Mars, rather than the Mercury mines. If…"

It was a big *if*, and a vague one. They needed men on Mars who could act as links in their information bureau, and be ready to work on their side when the expected trouble came. They wanted men who could serve them loyally, even without orders. If he did them enough service, they might let him back to Earth. If he caused trouble enough, they could still ship him to Mercury.

"And suppose nothing happens?" he asked.

"Then who cares? You're just lucky enough to be alive."

"And what makes you think I'm going to be a spy for Security?"

The other had shrugged. "Why not, Gordon? You've been a spy for a yellow scandal sheet. Why not for us?"

Gordon had been smart enough to realize that perhaps Security was right.

They were in the slums around the city now. Marsport had been settled faster than it was ready to receive. Temporary buildings had been thrown up, and then had remained, decaying into deathtraps. It wasn't a pretty view that visitors got as they first reached Mars. But nobody except the romantic fools had ever thought frontiers were pretty.

The drummer who had watched Gordon tear up his yellow stub moved forward now. "First time?" he asked.

Gordon nodded, mentally cataloguing the drummer as the cockroach type, midway between the small-businessman slug and the petty-crook spider types that weren't worth bothering with. But the other took it as interest.

"Been here dozens of times, myself. Risking your life just to go into Marsport. Why Congress doesn't clean it up, *I'll* never know!"

Gordon's mind switched to the readers in his bag. The cards were plastic, and should be good for a week or so of use before they showed wear. During that time, by playing it carefully, he should have his stake. Then, if the gaming tables here were as crudely run as an oldtimer he'd known on Earth had said, he could try a coup.

"...be at Mother Corey's soon," the fat little drummer babbled on. "Notorious—worst place on Mars. Take it from me, brother, that's something! Even the cops are afraid to go in there. See it? There, to your left!"

The name was vaguely familiar as one of the sore spots of Marsport. Bruce Gordon looked, and spotted the ragged building, half a mile outside the dome. It had been a rocket-maintenance hangar once, then had been turned into temporary dwelling for the first deportees, when Earth began flooding Mars. Now, seeming to stand by habit alone, it radiated desolation and decay.

He stood up, grabbing for his bag, and spinning the drummer aside. He jerked forward, and caught the driver's shoulder. "Getting off!"

The driver shrugged his hand away. "Don't be crazy, mister! They—" He turned, saw it was Gordon, and his face turned blank. "It's your life, buster," he said, and reached for the brake. "I'll give you five minutes to get into coveralls and helmet and out through the airlock."

Gordon needed less than that; he'd practiced all the way from Earth. The transparent plastic of the coveralls went on easily enough, and his hands found the seals quickly. He slipped his few possessions into a bag at his belt, slid the knife into a spring holster above his wrist, and picked up the bowl-shaped helmet. It seated on a plastic seal, and the little air compressor at his back began to hum, ready to turn the thin wisp of Mars' atmosphere into a barely breathable pressure. He tested the Marspeaker—an amplifier and speaker in another pouch, designed to raise the volume of his voice to a level where it would carry through even the air of Mars.

The driver swore at the lash of sound, and grabbed for the airlock switch.

Gordon moved down unpaved streets that zig-zagged along, thick with the filth of garbage and poverty—the part of Mars never seen in the newsreels, outside the shock movies. Thin kids with big eyes and sullen mouths crowded the streets in their airsuits, yelling profanity. The street was filled with people watching with a numbed hunger for any kind of excitement.

It was late afternoon, obviously. Men were coming from the few bus routes, lugging tools and lunch baskets, slumped and beaten from labor in the atomic plants, the Martian conversion farms, and the industries that had come inevitably where inefficiency was better than the high prices of imports. The saloons were doing well enough, apparently, from the number that streamed in through their airlock entrances. But Gordon saw one of the bartenders paying money to a thickset person with an arrogant sneer; he knew then that the few profits from the cheap beer were never going home with the man. Storekeepers in the cheap little shops had the same lines on their faces as they saw on those of their customers.

Poverty and misery were the keynotes here, rather than the evil half-world the drummer had babbled about. But to Gordon's trained eyes, there was plenty of outright rottenness, too.

He grimaced, grateful that the supercharger on his airsuit filtered out some of the smell which the thin air carried. He'd thought he was familiar with human misery from his own Earth slum background. But there was no attempt to disguise it here.

Ahead, Mother Corey's reared up—a huge, ugly half-cylinder of pitted metal and native bricks, showing the patchwork of decades, before repairs had been abandoned. There were no windows, though once there had been; and the front was covered with a big sign that spelled out *Condemned*. The airseal was filthy, and there was no bell.

Gordon kicked against the side, waited, and kicked again. A slit opened and closed. He waited, then drew his knife and began prying at the worn cement around the airseal, looking for the lock that had been there.

The seal suddenly quivered, indicating that metal inside had been withdrawn. Gordon grinned tautly, stepped through, and pushed the blade against the inner plastic.

"All right, all right," a voice whined out of the darkness. "You don't have to puncture my seal. You're in."

"Then call them off!"

A wheezing chuckle answered him, and a phosphor bulb glowed weakly, shedding some light on a filthy hall. "Okay, boys," the voice said, "come on down. He's alone, anyhow. What's pushing, stranger?"

"A yellow ticket," Gordon told him, "and a government allotment that'll last me two weeks in the dome. I figure on making it last six here, and don't let my being a firster give you hot palms. My brother was Lanny Gordon!"

It happened to be true, though Bruce Gordon hadn't seen his brother from the time the man had left the family, as a young punk, to the day they finally convicted him on his twenty-first murder. But here, if it was like places he'd known on Earth, even second-hand contact with "muscle" was useful.

It seemed to work. A huge man oozed out of the shadows, his gray face contorting its doughy fat into a yellow-toothed grin, and a filthy hand waved back the others. There were a few wisps of long, gray hair on the head and face, and they quivered as he moved forward.

"Looking for a room?" he whined.

"I'm looking for Mother Corey."

"Then you're looking at him, cobber. Sleep on the floor, want a bunk, squat with four, or room and duchess to yourself?"

There was a period of haggling, followed by a wait as Mother Corey kicked four grumbling men out of a four-by-seven hole on the second floor. Gordon's money had carried more weight than his brother's reputation; for that, Corey humored his guest's wish for privacy. "All yours, cobber, while your crackle's blue."

It was a filthy, dark place. In one corner was an unsheeted bed. There was a rusty bucket for water, a hole kicked through the floor for waste water. Plumbing, and such luxuries, apparently hadn't existed for years—except for the small cistern and worn water-recovery plant in the basement, beside the tired-looking weeds in the hydroponic tanks that tried unsuccessfully to keep the air breathable.

"What about a lock on the door?" Gordon asked.

"What good would it do you? Got a different way here, we have. One credit a week, and you get Mother Corey's word nobody busts in. And it sticks, cobber—one way or the other."

Gordon paid, and tossed his pouch on the filthy bed. With a little work, the place could be cleaned enough.

He pulled the cards out of his pouch, trying to be casual. Mother Corey stood staring at the pack while Bruce Gordon changed out of his airsuit, gagging faintly as the full effluvium of the place hit him. "Where does a man eat around here?"

Mother Corey pried his eyes off the cards and ran a thick tongue over heavy lips. "Eh? Oh. Eat. There's a place about ten blocks back. Cobber, stop teasing me! With elections coming up, and the boys loaded with vote money back in town—with a deck of cheaters like that—you want to *eat?*"

He picked the deck up fondly, while a faraway look came into his clouded eyes. "Same ones—same identical ones I wore out nigh twenty years ago. Smuggled two decks up here. Set to clean up—and I did, for a while." He shook his head sadly, and handed the deck back to Gordon. "Come on down. For the sight of these, I'll give you the lay for your pitch. And when your luck's made or broken, remember Mother Corey was your friend first, and your old Mother can get longer use from them than you can."

He waddled off, telling of his plans to take Mars for a cleaning, once long ago. Gordon followed him, staring at the surrounding filth.

His thoughts were churning so busily that he didn't see the blonde girl until she had forced her way past them on the stairs. Then he turned back, but she had vanished into one of the rooms.

CHAPTER TWO
Honest Izzy

A lot could be done in ten days, when a man knew what he was after. It was exactly ten days later. Bruce Gordon stood in the motley crowd inside the barnlike room where Fats ran a bar along one wall, and filled the rest of the space with assorted tables—all worn. Gordon was sweating slightly as he stood at the roulette table, where both zero and double-zero were reserved for the house.

The croupier was a little wizened man wanted on Earth. His eyes darted down to the point of the knife that showed under Gordon's sleeve, and he licked his lips, showing snaggled teeth. The wheel hesitated and came to a halt, with the ball trembling in a pocket.

"Twenty-one wins again." He pushed chips toward Gordon, as if every one of them came out of his own pay. "Place your bets."

Two others around the table watched narrowly as Gordon left his chips where they were; they then exchanged looks and shook their heads. In a Martian roulette game, numbers with that much riding just didn't turn up. The croupier shifted his weight, then caught the wheel and spun it savagely.

Gordon's leg ached from his strained position, but he shifted his weight onto it more heavily, and sweat popped out on the croupier's face. His eyes darted down, to where the full weight of Gordon seemed to rest on the heel that was grinding into his instep. He tried to pull his foot off the button that was concealed in the floor.

The heel ground harder, bringing a groan from him. And the ball hovered over Twenty-one and came to rest there once more.

Slowly, painfully, the little man counted stacks of chips and moved them across the table toward Gordon, his hands trembling.

Gordon straightened from his awkward position, drawing his foot back, and reached out for the pile of chips. Then he scooped it up and nodded. "Okay. I'm not greedy."

The strain of watching the games until he could spot the fix, and then holding the croupier down, had left him momentarily weak, but Gordon could still feel the tensing of the crowd. Now he let his eyes run over them—the night citizens of Marsport, lower-dome section. Spacemen who'd missed their ships; men who'd come here with dreams, and stayed without them—the shopkeepers who couldn't meet their graft and were here to try to win it on a last chance; street women and petty grifters. The air was thick with their unwashed bodies—all Mars smelled, since water was still too rare for frequent bathing—and their cheap perfume, and clouded with cheap Marsweed cigarettes.

Gordon swung where their eyes pointed, until he saw Fats Eller sidling through the groups, then let the knife slip into the palm of his hand as the crowd seemed to hold its breath. Fats plucked a sheaf of Martian bank notes from his pocket and tossed them to the croupier.

"Cash in his chips." Then his pouchy eyes turned to Gordon. "Get your money, punk, and get out! And stay out!"

For a moment, as he began pocketing the bills, Gordon thought he was going to get away that easily. Fats watched him dourly, then swung on his heel, just as a shrill, strangled cry went up from someone in the crowd.

The deportee let his glance jerk to it, then froze. His eyes caught the sight of a hand pointing behind him, and he knew it was too crude a trick to bother with. But he paused, shocked to see the girl he'd seen on Mother Corey's stairs gazing at him in well-feigned warning. In spite of his better judgment, she caught his eyes and drew them down over curves and swells that would always be right for arousing a man's passion.

He glanced back at Fats, who had started to turn again. Gordon took a step backwards, preparing to duck. Again the girl's finger motioned behind him; he disregarded it—and then realized it was a mistake.

It was the faintest swish in the air that caught his ear; he brought his shoulders up and his head down. Fast as his reaction was, it was almost too late. The weapon crunched against his shoulder and slammed over the back of his neck, almost knocking him out.

His heel lashed back and caught the shin of the man behind him. Gordon's other leg spun him around, still crouching; the knife in his hand started coming up, sharp edge leading, and aimed for the belly of the bruiser who confronted him. The pug saw the blade and tried to check his lunge.

Gordon felt the blade strike; but he was already pulling his swing, and it only gashed a long streak. The thug shrieked hoarsely and fell over. That left the way clear to the door; Bruce Gordon was through it and into the night in two soaring leaps. After only a few days on Mars, his legs were still hardened to Earth gravity, and he had more than a double advantage over the others.

Outside, it was the usual Martian night in the poorer section of the dome, which meant near-darkness. Most of the street lights had never been installed—graft had eaten up the appropriations, instead—and the nearest one was around the corner, leaving the side of Fats' Place in the shadow. Gordon checked his speed, threw himself flat, and rolled back against the building, just beyond the steps that led to the street.

Feet pounded out of the door above as Fats and the bouncer broke through. Gordon's hand had already knotted a couple of coins into his kerchief; he waited until the two turned uncertainly up the street and tossed it. It struck the wall near the corner, sailed on, and struck again at the edge of the unpaved street with a muffled sound.

Fats and the other swung, just in time to see a bit of dust where it had hit. "Around the corner!" Fats yelled. "After him, and shoot!"

In the shadows, Gordon jerked sharply. It was rare enough to have a gun here; but to use one inside the dome was unthinkable. His eyes shot up, to where the few dim lights were reflected off the great plastic sheet that was held up by air pressure and reinforced with heavy webbing. It was the biggest dome ever built—large enough to cover all of Marsport before the slums sprawled out beyond it; it still covered half the city, and made breathing possible here without a helmet. But the dome wasn't designed to stand stray bullets; and having firearms inside it—except for a few chosen men—was a crime punishable by death.

Fats had swung back, and was now herding the crowd inside his place. He might have been only a small gambling-house owner, but within his own circle his words carried weight.

Gordon got to his hands and knees and began crawling away from the corner. He came to a dark alley, smelling of decay where garbage had piled up without being carted away. Beyond lay a lighted street, and a sign that announced *Mooney's Amusement Palace—Drinks Free to Patrons!* He looked up and down the street, then walked briskly toward the somewhat plusher gambling hall there. Fats couldn't touch him in a competitor's place.

Inside Mooney's, he headed quickly for the dice table. He lost steadily on small bets for half an hour, admiring the skilled palming of the "odds" cubes. The loss was only a tiny dent in his new pile, but Gordon bemoaned it properly—as if he were broke—and moved over to the bar. This one had seats. The bartender had a consolation boilermaker waiting; he gulped half of it before he realized it had been needled with ether.

Beside him, a cop was drinking the same slowly, watching another policeman at a Canfield game. He was obviously winning, and now he got up and came over to cash in his chips.

"You'd think they'd lose count once in a while," he complained to his companion. "But nope—fifty even a night, no more... Well, come on, Pete. We'd better get back to Fats and tell him the swindler got away."

Gordon followed them out and turned south, down the street toward the edge of the dome and the entrance where he'd parked his airsuit and helmet. He kept glancing back, whenever he was in the thicker shadows, but there seemed to be no one following him.

At the gate of the dome, he looked back again, then ducked into the locker building. He threaded through the maze of the lockers with his knife ready in his hand, trying not to attract suspicion. At this hour, though, most of the place was empty. The crowds of foremen and deliverymen who'd be going in and out through the day were lacking.

He found his suit and helmet and clamped them on quickly, transferring the knife to its spring sheath outside the suit. He checked the tiny batteries that were recharged by generators in the soles of the boots with every step. Then he paid his toll for the opening of the private slit and went through, into the darkness outside the dome.

Lights bobbed about—police in pairs, patrolling in the better streets, walking as far from the houses as they could; a few groups, depending on numbers for safety; some of the very poor, stumbling about and hoping for a drink somehow; and probably hoods from the gangs that ruled the nights here.

Gordon left his torch unlighted, and moved along; there was a little illumination from the phosphorescent markers at some of the corners, and from the stars. He could just make his way without marking himself with a light.

Damn it, he should have hired a few of the younger bums from Mother Corey's. Here he couldn't hear footsteps. He located a pair of patrolling cops, and followed them down one street, until they swung off. Then he was on his own again.

"Gov'nor!" The word barely reached him, and Bruce Gordon spun around, the knife twitching into his hand. It was a thin kid of perhaps eighteen behind him, carrying a torch that was filtered to bare visibility. It swung up, and he saw a pock-marked face that was twisted in a smile meant to be ingratiating.

"You've got a pad on your tail," the kid said, again as low as his amplifier would permit. "Need a convoy?"

Gordon studied him briefly, and grinned. Then his grin wiped out as the kid's arm flashed to his shoulder and back, a series of quick jerks that seemed almost a blur. Four knives stood buried in the ground at Gordon's feet, forming a square—and a fifth was in the kid's hand.

"How much?" he asked, as the kid scooped up the blades and shoved them expertly back into shoulder sheaths. The kid's hand shaped a C quickly, and Gordon slipped his arm through a self-sealing slit in the airsuit and brought out two of them.

"Thanks, gov'nor," the kid said, stowing them away. "You won't regret it." Gordon started to turn. Then the kid's voice rose sharply to a yell. "Okay, honey, he's the Joe!"

Out of the darkness, ten to a dozen figures loomed up. The kid had jumped aside with a lithe leap, and now stood between Gordon and the group moving in for the kill. Gordon swung to run, and found himself surrounded. His eyes flickered around, trying to spot something in the darkness that would give him shelter.

A bludgeon was suddenly hurtling toward him, and he ducked it, his blood thick in his throat and his ears ringing with the same pressure of fear he'd always known just before he was kayoed in the ring. Then he selected what he hoped was the thinnest section of the attackers and leaped forward. With luck, he might jump over them, using his Earth strength.

There was a flicker of dawnlight in the sky, now, however; and he made out others behind, ready for just such a move. He changed his lunge in mid-stride, and brought his arm back with the knife. It met a small round shield on the arm of the man he had chosen, and was deflected at once.

"Give 'em hell, gov'nor," the kid's voice yelled, and the little figure was beside him, a shower of blades seeming to leap from his hand in the glare of his bare torch. Shields caught them frantically, and then the kid was in with a heavy club he'd torn from someone's hand.

Gordon had no time to consider his sudden traitor-ally. He bent to the ground, seizing the first rocks he could find, and threw them. One of the hoods dropped his club in ducking; Gordon caught it up and swung in a single motion that stretched the other out.

Then it was a melée. The kid's open torch, stuck on his helmet, gave them light enough, until Gordon could switch on his own. Then the kid dropped behind him, fighting back-to-back. Here, in close quarters, the attackers were no longer using knives. One might be turned on its owner, and a slit suit meant death by asphyxiation.

Gordon saw the blonde girl on the outskirts, her face taut and glowing. He tried to reach her with a thrown club wrested from another man, but she leaped nimbly aside, shouting commands.

Two burly goons were suddenly working together. Gordon swung at one, ducked a blow from the other, and then saw the first swinging again. He tried to bring his club up—but knew it was too late. A dull weight hit the side of his head, and he felt himself falling.

It took only minutes for dawn to become day on Mars, and the sun was lighting up the messy section of back street when Bruce Gordon's eyes opened and the pain of sight struck his aching head. He groaned, then looked frantically for the puff of escaping air. But his suit was still sealed. Ahead of him, the kid lay sprawled out, blood trickling from an ugly bruise along his jaw.

Then Gordon felt something on his suit, and his eyes darted to hands just finishing an emergency patch. His eyes darted up and met those of the blonde vixen!

Amazement kept him motionless for a second. There were tears in the eyes of the girl, and a sniffling sound reached him through her Marspeaker. Apparently, she hadn't noticed that he had revived, though her eyes were on him. She finished the patch, and ran perma-sealer over it. Then she began putting her supplies away, tucking them into a bag that held notes that could only have been stolen from his pockets—her share of the loot, apparently.

He was still thinking clumsily as she got to her feet and turned to leave. She cast a glance back, hesitated, and then began to move off.

He got his feet under him slowly, but he was reviving enough to stand the pain in his head. He came to his feet, and leaped after her. In the thin air, his lunge was silent, and he was grabbing her before she knew he was up.

She swung with a single gasp, and her hand darted down for her knife, sweeping it up and toward him; he barely caught the wrist coming toward him. Then he had her firmly, bringing her arm back and up, until the knife fell from her fingers.

She screamed and began writhing, twisting her hard young body like a boa constrictor in his hands. But he was stronger.

He bent her back over his knee, until a mangled moan was coming from her speaker; then his foot kicked out, knocking her feet out from under her. He let her hit the ground, caught both her wrists in his, and brought his knee down on her throat, applying more pressure until she lay still. Then he reached for the pouch.

"Damn you!" Her cry was more in anguish then it had been when he was threatening to break her back. "You damned firster, I'll kill you if it's the last thing I do. And after I saved your miserable life…"

"Thanks for that," he grunted. "Next time don't be a fool. When you kill a man for his money, he doesn't feel very grateful for your reviving him."

He started to count the money. About a tenth of what he had won—not even enough to open a cheap poker den, let alone bribe his way back to Earth.

The girl was out from under his knee at the first relaxation of pressure. Her hand scooped up the knife, and she came charging toward him, her mouth a taut slit across half-bared teeth. Gordon rolled out of her swing, and brought his foot up. It caught her squarely under the chin, and she went down and out.

He picked up the scattered money and her knife, then made sure she was still breathing. He ran his hands over her, looking for a hiding place for more money; there was none.

"Good work, gov'nor," the kid's thin voice approved, and Gordon swung to see the other getting up painfully. The kid grinned, rubbing his bruise. "No hard feelings, gov'nor, now! They paid me to stall you, so I did. You bonused me to protect you, and I bloody well tried. Honest Izzy, that's me. Gonna buy me a job as a cop. That's why I needed the scratch. Okay, gov'nor?"

Gordon hauled back his hand to knock the other from his feet, and then dropped it. A grin writhed onto his face, and broke into sudden grudging laughter.

"Okay, Izzy," he admitted. "For this stinking planet, I guess you're something of a saint. Come along, and we'll both apply for that job—after I get my stuff."

He might as well join the law. Security had wanted him to police their damned planet for them—and he might as well do it officially.

He tossed the girl's knife down beside her, motioned to Izzy, and began heading for Mother Corey's.

CHAPTER THREE
The Graft is Green

Izzy seemed surprised when he found that Gordon was turning in to the quasi-secret entrance to Mother Corey's. "Coming here myself," he explained. "Mother got ahold of a load of snow, and sent me out to contact a big pusher. Coming back, the goons picked me up and gave me the job on you. Hey, Mother!"

Bruce Gordon didn't ask how Mother Corey had acquired the dope. When Earth had deported all addicts two decades before, it had practically begged for dope smuggling.

The gross hulk of Mother Corey appeared almost at once. "Izzy and Bruce. Didn't know you'd met, cobbers. Contact, Izzy?"

"Ninety per cent for uncut," Izzy answered.

They went up to Gordon's hole-in-the-wall, with Mother Corey wheezing behind, while the rotten wood of the stairs groaned under his grotesque bulk. At his questions, Gordon told the story tersely.

Mother Corey nodded. "Same old angles, eh? Get enough to do the job, they mug you. Stop halfway, and the halls are closed to you. Pretty soon, they'll be trick-proof, anyhow; they're changing over to electric eyes. Eh, you haven't forgotten me, cobber?"

Gordon hadn't. The old wreck had demanded five per cent of his winnings for tipping him off. Mother Corey had too many cheap hoods among his friends to be fooled with. Gordon counted out the money reluctantly, while Izzy explained that they were going to be cops.

The old man shook his head, estimating what was left to Gordon. "Enough to buy a corporal's job, pay for your suit, and maybe get by," he decided. "Don't do it, cobber. You're the wrong kind. You take what you're doing serious. When you set out to tinhorn a living, you're a crook. Get you in a cop's outfit, and you'll turn honest. No place here for an honest cop—not with elections coming up, cobber. Well, I guess you gotta find out for yourself. Want a good room?"

Gordon's lips twitched. "Thanks, Mother, but I'll be staying inside the dome, I guess."

"So'll I," the old man gloated. "Setting in a chair all day, being an honest citizen. Cobber, I already own a joint there— a nice one, they tell me. Lights. Two water closets. Big rooms, six-by-ten—fifty of them, big enough for whole families. And strictly on the level, cobber. It's no hide-out, like this."

He rolled the money in his greasy fingers. "Now, with what I get from the pusher, I can buy off that hot spot on the police blotter. I can go in the dome and walk around, just like you." His eyes watered, and a tear went dripping down his nose. "I'm getting old. They'll be calling me 'Grandmother' pretty soon. So I'm turning my Chicken House over to my granddaughter and I'm going honest. Want a room?"

Gordon grinned, and nodded. Mother Corey knew the ropes, and could be trusted. "Didn't know you had a granddaughter."

Izzy snorted, and Mother Corey grinned wolfishly. "You met her, cobber. The blonde you shook down! Came up from Earth eight years ago, looking for me. I sold her to the head of the East Point gang. Since she killed him, she's been doing pretty well on her own. Mostly. Except when she makes a fool of herself, like she did with you. But she'll come around to where I'm proud of her, yet... If you two want to carry in the snow, collect, and turn it over to Commissioner Arliss for me—I can't pass the dome till he gets it—I'll give you both rooms for six months free. Except for the lights and water, of course."

Izzy nodded, and Gordon shrugged. On Mars, it didn't seem odd to begin applying for a police job by carrying in narcotics. He wondered how they'd go about contacting the commissioner.

But that turned out to be simple enough. After collecting, Izzy led the way into a section marked "Special Taxes" and whispered a few casual words. The man at the desk went into an office marked private, and came back a few minutes later.

"Your friend has no record with us," he said in a routine voice. "I've checked through his tax forms, and they're all in order. We'll confirm officially, of course."

In the Applications section of the big Municipal Building, at the center of the dome, there was a long form to fill out at the desk; but the captain there had already had answers typed in.

"Save time, boys," he said genially. "And time's valuable, ain't it? Ah, yes." He took the sums they had ready—there was a standard price—and stamped their forms. "And you'll want suits. Isaacs? Good, here's your receipt. And you, Corporal Gordon. Right. Get your suits one floor down, end of the hall. And report in eight tomorrow morning!"

It was as simple as that. Bruce Gordon was lucky enough to get a fair fit in his suit. He'd almost forgotten what it felt like to be in uniform.

Izzy was more businesslike. "Hope they don't give us too bad territory, gov'nor," he remarked. "Pickings are always a little lean on the first few beats, but you can work some fairly well."

Gordon's chest fell; this was Mars!

The room at the new Mother Corey's—an unkempt old building near the edge of the dome—proved to be livable, though it was a shock to see Mother Corey himself in a decent suit, and using perfume.

The beat was in a shabby section where clerks and skilled laborers worked. It wasn't poor enough to offer the universal desperation that gave the gang hoodlums protective coloring, nor rich enough to have major rackets of its own.

Izzy was disgusted. "Cripes! Hope they've got a few cheap pushers around that don't pay protection direct to the captain. You take that store; I'll go in this one!"

The proprietor was a druggist who ran his own fountain where the synthetics that replaced honest Earth foods were compounded into sweet and sticky messes for the neighborhood kids. He looked up as Gordon came in; then his face fell. "New cop, eh? No wonder Gable collected yesterday, ahead of time. All right, you can look at my books. I've been paying fifty, but you'll have to wait until Friday."

Gordon nodded and swung on his heel, surprised to find that his stomach was turning. The man obviously couldn't afford fifty credits a week. But it was the same all along the street. Even Izzy admitted finally that they'd have to wait.

"That damned cop before us! He really tapped them! And we can't take less, so I guess we gotta wait until Friday."

The next day, Bruce Gordon made his first arrest. It was near the end of his shift, just as darkness was falling and the few lights were going on. He turned a corner and came to a short, heavy hoodlum backing out of a small liquor store with a knife in throwing position. The crook grunted as he started to turn and stumbled onto Gordon. His knife flashed up.

Without the need to worry about an airsuit, Gordon moved in, his arm jerking forward. He clipped the crook on the inside of the elbow, while grabbing the wrist with his other hand. The man went sailing over Gordon's head, to crash into the side of the building. He let out a yell.

Gordon rifled the hood's pockets, and located a roll of bills stuffed in. He dragged them out, before snapping cuffs on the man. Then he pulled the crook inside the store.

A woman stood there, moaning over a pale man on the floor; blood oozed from a welt on the back of his head. There was both gratitude and resentment as she looked up at Gordon.

"You'd better call the hospital," he told her sharply. "He may have a concussion. I've got the man who held you up."

"Hospital?" Her voice broke into another wail. "And who can afford hospitals? All week we work, all hours. He's old, he can't handle the cases. I do that. Me! And then you come, and you get your money. And *he* comes for his protection. Papa is sick. Sick, do you hear? He sees a doctor, he buys medicine. Then Gable comes. This man comes. We can't pay him! So what do we get—we get knifes in the faces, saps on the head—a concussion, you tell me! And all the money—the money we had to pay to get stocks to sell to pay off from the profits we don't make—all of it, he wants! Hospitals! You think they give away at the hospitals free?"

She fell to her knees, crying over the injured man.

Gordon tossed the roll of bills onto the floor beside her; the injury seemed only a scalp wound, and the old man was already beginning to groan. He opened his eyes and saw the bills in front of him, at which the woman was staring unbelievingly. His hand darted out, clutching it. "God!" he moaned softly, and his eyes turned up slowly to Gordon.

"In there!" It was a shout from outside. Gordon had just time to straighten up before the doorway was filled with two knife-men and a heavier one behind them.

His hands dropped to the handcuffed man on the floor, and he caught him up with a jerk, slapping his body back against the counter. He took a step forward, jerking his hands up and putting his Earth-adapted shoulders behind it. The hood sailed up and struck the two knife-men squarely.

There was a scream as their automatic attempts to save themselves buried both knives in the body of their friend. Then they went crashing down, and Gordon was over them.

The desk captain at the precinct house groaned as they came in, then shook his head. "Damn it," he said. "I suppose it can't be helped, though; you're new, Gordon. Hennessy, get the corpse to the morgue, and mark it down as a robbery attempt. I'm going to have to book you and your men, Mr. Jurgens!"

The heavy leader of the two angry knife-men grinned. "Okay, Captain. But it's going to slow down the work I'm doing on the Mayor's campaign for re-election! Damn that Maxie—I told him to be discreet. Hey, you know what you've got, though—a real considerate man! He gave the old guy his money back!"

They took Bruce Gordon's testimony, and sent him home.

Jurgens was waiting for him when he came on the beat. From his look of having slept well, he must have been out almost as soon as he was booked. Two other men stood behind Gordon, while Jurgens explained that he didn't like being interrupted on business calls "about the Mayor's campaign, or anything else," and that next time there'd be real hard feelings. Gordon was surprised when he wasn't beaten, but not when the racketeer suggested that any money found at a crime was evidence and should go to the police. The captain had told him the same.

By Friday, he had learned. He made his collections early. Gable had sold him the list of what was expected, and he used it, though he cut down the figures in a few cases. There was no sense in killing the geese that laid the eggs.

The couple at the liquor store had their payment waiting, and they handed it over, looking embarrassed. It wasn't until he was gone that he found a small bottle of fairly good whiskey tucked into his pouch. He started to throw it away, and then lifted it to his lips. Maybe they'd known how he felt better than he had. Mother Corey's words about his change of attitude came back. Damn it, he had to dig up enough money to get back to Earth.

He collected, down to the last account. It was a nice haul; at that rate, he'd have to stand it only for a few months. Then Gordon's lips twisted, as he realized it wasn't all gravy. There were angles, or the price of a corporalcy would have been higher.

One of the older men answered his questions. "Fifty per cent of the take to the Orphan's and Widow's fund. Better make it more than Gable turned in, if you want to get a better beat."

The envelopes were lying on a table marked "Voluntary Donations"; Gordon filled his out, with a figure a bit higher than half of Gable's take, and dropped it in the box. The captain, who had been watching him carefully, settled back and smiled.

"Widows and Orphans sure appreciate a good man," he said. "I was kind of worried about you, Gordon, but you got a nice touch. One of my new boys—Isaacs, you know him— was out checking up after you, and the dopes seem to like you."

Gordon had wondered why Izzy had been pulled off the beat. As he turned to leave, the captain held up a hand. "Special meeting tomorrow. We gotta see about getting out a good vote. Election only three weeks away."

Gordon went home. He'd learned by now that the native Martians—those who'd been here for at least thirty years, or had been born here—were backing a reform candidate and new ticket. But Mayor Wayne had all of the rest of the town in his hand. He'd been in twice, and had lifted the graft take by a truly remarkable figure. From where Gordon stood, it looked like a clear victory for the reformer, Nolan.

He went into the meeting willing to agree to anything. He applauded all the speeches about how much Mayor Wayne had done for them, and signed the pledge expressing his confidence, along with the implied duty he had to make his beat vote right. Then he stopped, as the captain stood up.

"We gotta be neutral, boys," he boomed. "But it don't mean we can't show how well we like the Mayor. Just remember, he got us our jobs! Now I figure we can all kick in a little to help his campaign. I'm going to start it off with five thousand credits, two thousand of them right now."

They fell in line, though there was no cheering. The price might have been fixed in advance. A thousand for a plain cop, fifteen hundred for a corporal, and so on, each contributing a third of it now. Gordon grimaced; he had six hundred left. This would take nearly all of it.

A man named Fell shook his head, fearfully. "Can't do a thing now. My wife had a baby and an operation, and—"

"Okay, Fell," the captain said, without a sign of disapproval. "Freitag, what about you? Fine, fine!"

Gordon's name came, and he shook his head. "I'm new—and I'm strapped now. I'd like—"

"Quite all right, Gordon," the captain boomed. "Harwick!"

He finished the roll, and settled back, smiling. "I guess that's all, boys. Thanks from the Mayor. And go on home... Oh, Fell, Gordon, Lativsky—stick around. I've got some overtime for you, since you need extra money. The boys out in Ward Three are shorthanded. Afraid I'll have to order you out there!"

Ward Three was the hangout of a cheap gang of hoodlums, numbering some four hundred, who went in for small crimes mostly. But they had recently declared war on the cops.

After eight hours of overtime, Gordon reported in with every bone sore from small missiles, and his suit filthy from assorted muck. He had a beautiful shiner where a stone had clipped him.

The captain smiled. "Rough, eh? But I hear robbery went down on your beat last night. Fine work, Gordon. We need men like you. Hate to do it, but I'm afraid you'll have to take the next shift at Main and Broad, directing traffic. The usual man is sick, and you're the only one I can trust with the job!"

Gordon stuck it out, somehow, but it wasn't worth it. He reported back to the precinct with the five hundred in his hand, and his pen itching for the donation agreement.

The captain took it, and nodded. "I wasn't kidding about your being a good man, Gordon. Go home and get some sleep, take the next day off. After that, we've got a new job for you!"

CHAPTER FOUR
Captain Murcoch

The new assignment was to the roughest section in all Marsport—the slum area beyond the dome, out near the rocket field. Here all the riffraff that had been unable to establish itself in better quarters had found some sort of a haven. At one time, there had been a small dome and a tiny city devoted to the rocket field. But Marsport had flourished enough to kill it off. The dome had failed from neglect, and the buildings inside had grown shabbier.

Bruce Gordon was trapped; he couldn't break his job with the police—if he did, he'd be brought back as a criminal. Some of Mars' laws dated from the time when law enforcement had been hampered by lack of men, rather than by the type of men.

The Stonewall gang numbered perhaps five hundred. They hired out members to other gangs, during the frequent wars. Between times, they picked up what they could by mugging and theft, with a reasonable amount of murder thrown in at a modest price.

Even derelicts and failures had to eat; there were stores and shops throughout the district which eked out some kind of a marginal living. They were safe from protection racketeers there—none bothered to come so far out. And police had been taken off the beats there after it grew unsafe even for men in pairs to patrol the area.

The shopkeepers, and some of the less unfortunate people there, had protested loud enough to reach clear back to Earth. Marsport had hired a man from Earth to come in and act as chief of the section. Captain Murdoch was an unknown factor, and now was asking for more men. The pressure was enough to get them for him.

Gordon reported for work with a sense of the bottom falling out, mixed with a vague relief.

"You're going to be busy," Murdoch announced shortly in the dilapidated building that had been hastily converted to a precinct house. "Damn it, you're men, not sharks. I've got a free hand, and we're going to run this the way we would on Earth. Your job is to protect the citizens here—and that means everyone not breaking the laws—whether you feel like it or not. No graft. The first man making a shakedown will get the same treatment we're going to use on the Stonewall boys. You'll get double pay here, and you can live on it!"

He opened up a box on his desk and pulled out six heavy wooden sticks, each thirty inches long and nearly two inches in diameter. There was a shaped grip on each, with a thong of leather to hold it over the wrist.

He picked out five of the men, including Gordon "You five will come with me. I'm going to show how we operate. The rest of you can team up any way you want tonight, pick any route that's open. Okay, men, let's go."

Bruce Gordon grinned slowly as he swung the stick, and Murdoch's eyes fell on him. "Earth cop!"

"Two years," Gordon admitted.

"Then you should be ashamed to be in this mess. But whatever your reasons, you'll be useful. Take those two and give them some lessons, while I do the same with these."

For a second, Gordon cursed himself. Murdoch had fixed it so he'd be a squad leader, and that meant he'd be unable to step out of line. At double standard pay, with normal Mars expenses, he might be able to pay for passage back to Earth in three years—if Security let him. Otherwise, it would take thirty.

He began wondering about Security, then. Nobody had tried to get in touch with him. Were they waiting for him to get up on a soapbox?

There was a crude lighting system here, put up by the citizens. At the front of each building, a dim phosphor bulb glowed; when darkness fell, they would have nothing else to see by.

Murdoch bunched them together. "A good clubbing beats hanging," he told them. "But it has to be *good*. Go in for business, and don't stop just because the other guy quits. Give them hell!"

Moving in two groups of threes, at opposite sides of the street, they began their beat. They were covering an area of six blocks one way, and two the other.

They had traveled the six blocks and were turning down a side street when they found their first case; it was still daylight. Two of the Stonewall boys were working over a tall man in a newer airsuit. As the police swung around, one of the thugs casually ripped the airsuit open.

A thin screech like a whistle came from Murdoch's Marspeaker, and the captain went forward, with Gordon at his heels. The hoodlums tossed the man aside easily, and let out a yell. From the buildings around, an assortment of toughs came at the double, swinging knives, picks, and bludgeons.

There was no chance to save the citizen, who was dying from lack of air. Gordon felt the solid pleasure of the finely turned club in his hands. It was light enough for speed, but heavy enough to break bones where it hit. A skilled man could knock a knife, or even a heavy club, out of another's hand with a single flick of the wrist. And he'd had practice.

He saw Murdoch's club dart in and take out two of the gang, one on the forward swing, one on the recover. Gordon's eyes popped at that. The man was totally unlike a Martian captain, and a knot of homesickness for Earth ran through his stomach.

He swallowed the sentiment; his own club was moving now. Standing beside Murdoch, they were moving forward. The other four cops had come in reluctantly.

"Knock them out and kick them down!" Murdoch yelled. "And don't let them get away!"

Gordon was after a thug who was attempting to run away. He brought him to the ground with a single blow across the kidneys.

It was soon over. They rounded up the men of the gang, and one of the cops started off. Murdoch called, "Where are you going?"

"To find a phone and call the wagon."

"We're not using wagons," Murdoch told him. "Line them up."

When the hoods came to, they found themselves helpless, and facing police with clubs. If they tried to run, they were hit from behind; if they stood still, they were clubbed carefully. If they fought back, the pugnaciousness was knocked out of them at once.

Murdoch indicated one who stood with his shoulders shaking and tears running down his cheeks. The captain's face was as sick as Gordon felt. "Take him aside. Names."

Gordon found a section away from the others. "I want the name of every man in the gang you can remember," he told the man.

Horror shot over the other's bruised features. "Colonel, they'd kill me! I don't know."

His screams were almost worse than the beating but names began to come. Gordon took them down, and then returned with the man to the others.

Murdoch took his nod as evidence enough, and turned to the wretched toughs. "He squealed," he announced. "If he should turn up dead, I'll know you boys are responsible, and I'll find you. Now get out of this district, or get honest jobs! Because every time one of my men sees one of you, this will happen again. And you can pass the word along that the Stonewall gang is dead!"

He turned and moved off down the street, the others at his side. Gordon nodded. "I've heard the theory, but never saw it in practice. Suppose the whole gang jumps us at once?"

Murdoch shrugged. "Then we're taken. The old book I got the idea from didn't mention that."

Trouble began brewing shortly after, though. Men stood outside, studying the cops on their beat. Murdoch sent one of the men to pick up a second squad of six, and then a third. After that, the watchers began to melt away.

"We'd better shift to another territory," Murdoch decided. Gordon realized that the gang had figured that concentrating the police here meant other territories would be safe.

Two more groups were given the treatment. In the third one, Bruce Gordon spotted one of the men who'd been beaten before. He was a sick-looking spectacle.

Murdoch nodded. "Object lesson!"

The one good thing about the captain, Gordon decided, was that he believed in doing his own dirtiest work. When he was finished, he turned to two of the other captives.

"Get a stretcher, and take him wherever he belongs," he ordered. "I'm leaving you two able to walk for that. But if *you* get caught again, you'll get still worse."

The squad went in, tired and sore; all had taken a severe beating in the brawls. But there was little grumbling. Gordon saw grudging admiration in their eyes for Murdoch, who had taken more punishment than they had.

Gordon rode back in the official car with Murdoch and both were silent most of the way. But the captain stirred finally, sighing. "Poor devils!"

Gordon jerked up in surprise. "The gang?"

"No, the cops they're giving me. We're covered, Gordon. But the Stonewall gang is backing Wayne. He's let me come in because he figures it will get him more votes. But afterwards, he'll have me out; and then the boys with me will be marks for the gang when it comes back. Besides, it'll show on the books that they didn't kick into his fund. I can always go back to Earth, and I'll try to take you along. But it's going to be tough on them."

Bruce Gordon grimaced. "I've got a yellow ticket, from Security."

Murdoch blinked. He dropped his eyes slowly. "So you're that Gordon? But you're still a good cop."

They rode on further in silence, until Gordon broke the ice to ease the tension. He found himself liking the other.

"What makes you think Wayne will be re-elected? Nobody wants him, except a gang of crooks and those in power."

Murdoch grinned bitterly. "Ever see a Martian election? No, you're a firster. He can't lose! And then hell is going to pop, and this whole planet may be blown wide open!"

It fitted with the dire predictions of Security, and with the spying Gordon was going to do—according to them.

He discussed it with Mother Corey, who agreed that Wayne would be re-elected.

"Can't lose," the old man said. He was getting even fatter, now that he was eating better food from the fair restaurant around the corner.

"He'll win," Mother Corey repeated. "And you'll turn honest all over, now you're in uniform. Take me, cobber. I figured on laying low for a while, then opening up a few rooms for a good pusher or two, maybe a high-class duchess. Cost 'em more, but they'd be respectable. Only now I'm respectable myself, they don't look so good. But this honesty stuff, it's like dope. You start out on a little, and you have to go all the way."

"It didn't affect Honest Izzy," Gordon pointed out.

"Nope. Because Izzy is always honest, according to how he sees it. But you got Earth ideas of the stuff, like I had once. Too bad." He sighed ponderously.

The week moved on. The groups grew more experienced, and Murdoch was training a new squad every night. Gordon's own squad was equipped with shields now, and they were doing better. The number of muggings and holdups in the section was going down. They seldom saw a man after he'd been treated.

One of the squads was jumped by a gang of about forty, and two of the men were killed before the nearest other squad could pull a rear attack. That day the whole force worked overtime hunting for the men who had escaped; and by evening the Stonewall boys had received proof that it didn't pay to go against the police in large numbers.

After that, they began to go hunting for the members of the gang. They had the names of nearly all of them, and some pretty good ideas of their hide-outs.

It wasn't exactly legal; but nothing was, here. If a doctor's job was to prevent illness, instead of merely curing it, then why shouldn't it be a policeman's job to prevent crime? Here, that was best done by wiping out the Stonewall gang to the last member.

This could lead to abuses, as he'd seen on Earth. But there probably wouldn't be time for it if Mayor Wayne was re-elected.

The gang had begun to break up, but the nucleus would be the last to go. The police had orders to beat any member on sight, now. Citizens were appearing on the streets at night for the first time in years. And there were smiles—hungry, beaten smiles, but still genuine ones—for the cops.

CHAPTER FIVE
Recall

It was night outside, and the phosphor bulbs at the corners glowed dimly, giving him barely enough light by which to locate the way to the extemporized precinct house. Bruce Gordon reached the outskirts of the miserable business section, noticing that a couple of the shops were still open. It had probably been years since any had dared risk it after the sun went down. And the slow, doubtful respect on the faces of the citizens as they nodded to him was even more proof that Haley's system was working. Gordon nodded to a couple, and they grinned faintly at him. Damn it, Mars could be cleaned up...

He grinned at himself, then something needled at his mind, until he swung back. The man who had just passed was carrying a lunch basket, and was wearing the coveralls of one of the crop-prospector crews; but the expression on his face had been wrong.

Red hair, too heavily built, a lighter section where a mustache had been shaved and the skin not quite perfectly powdered... Gordon moved forward quickly, until he could make out the thin scar showing through the make-up over the man's eyes. He'd been right—this was O'Neill, head of the Stonewall gang.

Gordon hit the signal switch, and the Marspeaker let out a shrill whistle. O'Neill had turned to run, and then seemed to think better of it. His hand darted down to his belt, just as Gordon reached him.

The heavy locust stick met the man's wrist before the weapon was half drawn—another gun! Guns suddenly seemed to be flourishing everywhere. The gun dropped from O'Neill's hand as the wrist snapped, and the Stonewall chief let out a high-pitched cry of pain. Then another cop came around a corner at a run.

"You can't do it to me! I'm reformed; I'm going straight! You damned cops can't..." O'Neill was blubbering. The small crowd that was collecting was all to the good, Gordon knew, and he let O'Neill go on. Nothing could help break up the gangs more than having a leader break down in public.

The other cop had yanked out O'Neill's wallet, and now tossed it to Gordon. One look was enough—the work papers had the telltale over-thickening of the signature that had showed up on other papers, obviously forgeries. The cops had been passing them on the hope of finding one of the leaders.

Some turned away as Gordon and the other cop went to work, but most of them weren't squeamish. When it was over, the two picked up their whimpering captive. Gordon pocketed the revolver with his free hand. "Walk, O'Neill!" he ordered. "Your legs are still whole. Use them!"

The man staggered between them, whimpering at each step. If any members of the gang were around, they made no attempt to rescue him.

Jenkins, the other cop, had been holding the wallet. Now he held it out toward Gordon. "The gee was heeled, Corporal. Must of been making a big contact in something. Fifty-fifty?"

"Turn it in to Murdoch," Gordon said, and then cursed himself. There must have been over two thousand credits in the wallet.

The captain's face had been buried in a pile of papers, but now Murdoch came around to stare at the gang leader. He inspected the forged work papers, and jerked his thumb toward one of the hastily built cells where a doctor would look O'Neill over—eventually. When Gordon and Jenkins came back, Murdoch tossed the money to them. "Split it. You guys earned it by keeping your hands off it. Anyhow, you're as entitled to it as he was—or the grafters back at Police Headquarters. I never saw it. Gordon, you've got a visitor!"

His voice was bitter, but he made no opening for them to question him as he picked up the papers and began going through them again. Gordon went down the passage to the end of the hall, in the direction Murdoch had indicated. Waiting for him was the lean, cynical little figure of Honest Izzy, complete with uniform and sergeant's stripes.

"Hi, gov'nor," the little man greeted him. "Long time no see. With you out here and me busy nights doing a bit of convoy work on the side, we might as well not both live at Mother's."

Bruce Gordon nodded, grinning in spite of himself. "Convoy duty, Izzy? Or dope running?"

"Whatever comes to hand, gov'nor. The Force pays for my time during the day, and I figure my time's my own at night. Of course, if I ever catch myself doing anything shady during the day, I'll have to turn myself in. But it ain't likely." He grinned in satisfaction. "Now that I've dug up the scratch to buy these stripes and get made sergeant—and that takes the real crackle—I'm figuring on taking it easy."

"Like this social call?" Gordon asked him.

The little man shook his head, his ancient eighteen-year-old face turning sober. "Nope. I've been meaning to see you, so I volunteered to run out some red tape for your captain. You owe me some bills, gov'nor. Eleven hundred fifty credits. You didn't pay up your pledge to the campaign fund, so I hadda fill in. A thousand, interest at ten per cent a week, standard. Right?"

Gordon had heard of the friendly interest charged on the side here, but he shook his head. "Wrong, Izzy. If they want to collect that dratted pledge of theirs, let them put me where I can make it. There's no graft out here."

"Huh?" Izzy turned it over, and shook his head. Finally he shrugged. "Don't matter, gov'nor. Nothing about that in the pledge, and when you sign something, you gotta pay it. You *gotta.*"

"All right," Gordon admitted. He was suddenly in no mood to quibble with Izzy's personal code. "So you paid it. Now show me where I signed any agreement saying I'd pay *you* back!"

For a second, Izzy's face went blank; then he chuckled. "Jet me! You're right, gov'nor. I sure asked for that one. Okay; I'm bloody well suckered, so forget it."

Gordon shrugged and gave up. He pulled out the bills and handed them over. "Thanks, Izzy."

"Thanks, yourself." The kid pocketed the money cheerfully, nodding. "Buy you a beer. Anyhow, you won't miss it. I came out to tell you I got the sweetest beat in Marsport—over a dozen gambling joints on it—and I need a right gee to work it with me. So you're it!"

For a moment, Gordon wondered what Izzy had done to earn that beat, but he could guess. The little guy knew Mars as few others did, apparently, from all sides. And if any of the other cops had private rackets of their own, Izzy was undoubtedly the man to find it out, and use the information. With a beat such as that, even going halves, and with all the graft to the upper brackets, he'd still be able to make his pile in a matter of months.

But he shook his head. "I'm assigned here, Izzy, at least for another week, until after elections…"

"Better take him up, Gordon," Murdoch told him bitterly. The captain looked completely beaten as he came into the room and dropped onto the bench. "Go on, accept, damn it. You're not assigned here any more. None of us are. Mayor Wayne found an old clause in the charter and got a rigged decision, pulling me back under his full authority. I thought I had full responsibility to Earth, but he's got me. Wearing their uniform makes me a temporary citizen! So we're being smothered back into the Force, and they'll have their patsies out here, setting things up for the Stonewall boys to come back by election time. So grab while the grabbing's good, because by tomorrow morning I'll have this all closed down!"

He shook off Gordon's hand and stood up roughly, to head back up the hallway. Then he stopped and looked back. "One thing, though, I've still got enough authority to make you a sergeant. It's been a pleasure working with you, Sergeant Gordon!"

He swung out of view abruptly, leaving Gordon with a heavy weight in his stomach. Izzy whistled, and began picking up his helmet, preparing to go outside. "So that's the dope I brought out, eh? Takes it kind of hard, doesn't he?"

"Yeah," Gordon answered. There was no use trying to explain it to Izzy. "Yeah, we do. Come on."

Outside, Gordon saw other cops moving from house to house, and he realized that Murdoch must be sending out warnings to the citizens that things would soon be rough again.

Izzy held out a hand to Gordon. "Let's get a beer, gov'nor—on me!"

It was as good an idea as any he had, Gordon decided. He might as well enjoy what life he still had while he could. The Stonewall gang—what was left of it—and all its friends would be gunning for him now. The Force wouldn't have been fooled when Izzy paid his pledge, and they'd mark him down as disloyal—if they didn't automatically mark down all who'd served under Murdoch. And he didn't have the ghost of an idea as to what Security wanted of him, or where they were hiding themselves.

"Make it two beers, Izzy," he said. "Needled!"

CHAPTER SIX
Sealed Letter

In the few days at the short-lived Nineteenth Precinct, Bruce Gordon had begun to feel like a cop again, but the feeling disappeared as he reported in at Captain Isaiah Trench's Seventh Precinct. Trench had once been a colonel in the Marines, before a court-martial and sundry unpleasantnesses had driven him off Earth. His dark, scowling face and lean body still bore a military air.

He looked Bruce Gordon over sourly. "I've been reading your record. It stinks. Making trouble for Jurgens—could have been charged as false arrest. No co-operation with your captain until he forced it; out in the sticks beating up helpless men. Now you come crawling back to your only friend, Isaacs. Well, I'll give it a try. But step out of line and I'll have you cleaning streets with your bare hands. All right, *Corporal* Gordon. Dismissed. Get to your beat."

Gordon grinned wryly at the emphasis on his title. No need to ask what had happened to Murdoch's recommendation. He joined Izzy in the locker room, summing up the situation.

"Yeah." Izzy looked worried, his thin face pinched in. "Maybe I didn't do you a favor, gov'nor, pulling you here. I dunno. I got some pics of Trench from a guy I know. That's how I got my beat so fast in the Seventh. But Trench ain't married, and I guess I've used up the touch. Maybe I could try it, though."

"Forget it," Gordon told him. "I'll work it out somehow."

The beat was a gold mine. It lay through the section where Gordon had first tried his luck on Mars. There were a dozen or so gambling joints, half a dozen cheap saloons, and a fair number of places listed as rooming houses, though they made no bones about the fact that all their permanent inhabitants were female. Then the beat swung off, past a row of small businesses and genuine rooming houses, before turning back to the main section.

They began in the poorer section. It wasn't the day to collect the "tips" for good service, which had been an honest attempt to promote good police service before it became a racket. But they were met everywhere by sullen faces. Izzy explained it. The city had passed a new poll tax—to pay for election booths, supposedly—and had made the police collect it. Murdoch must have disregarded the order, but the rest of the force had been busy helping the administration.

But once they hit the main stem, things were mere routine. The gambling joints took it for granted that beat cops had to be paid, and considered it part of their operating expense. The only problem was that Fats' Place was the first one on the list. Gordon didn't expect to be too welcome there.

There was no sign of the thug, but Fats came out of his back office just as Gordon reached the little bar. He came over, nodded, picked up a cup and dice and began shaking them.

"High man for sixty," he said automatically, and expertly rolled bull's-eyes for a two. "Izzy said you'd be around. Sorry my man drew that *knife* on you the last time, Corporal."

Gordon rolled an eight, pocketed the bills, and shrugged. "Accidents will happen, Fats."

"Yeah." The other picked up the dice and began rolling sevens absently. "How come you're walking beat, anyhow? With what you pulled here, you should have bought a captaincy."

Gordon told him briefly. The man chuckled grimly. "Well, that's Mars," he said, and turned back to his private quarters.

Mostly, it was routine work. They came on a drunk later, collapsed in an alley. But the muggers had apparently given up before Izzy and Gordon arrived, since the man had his wallet clutched in his hand. Gordon reached for it, twisting his lips.

Izzy stopped him. "It ain't honest, gov'nor. If the gees in the wagon clean him, or the desk man gets it, that's their business. But I'm going to run a straight beat, or else!"

That was followed by a call to remove a berserk spaceman from one of the so-called rooming houses. Gordon noticed that workmen were busy setting up a heavy wooden gate in front of the entrance to the place. There were a lot of such preparations going on for the forthcoming elections.

Then the shift was over. But Gordon wasn't too surprised when his relief showed up two hours late; he'd half-expected some such nastiness from Trench. But he was surprised at the look on his tardy relief's face.

The man seemed to avoid facing him, muttered, "Captain says report in person at once," and swung out of the scooter and onto his beat without further words.

Gordon was met there by blank faces and averted looks, but someone nodded toward Trench's office, and he went inside. Trench sat chewing on a cigar. "Gordon, what does Security want with you?"

"Security? Not a damned thing, if I can help it. They kicked me off Earth on a yellow ticket, if that's what you mean."

"Yeah." Trench shoved a letter forward; it bore the "official business" seal of Solar Security, and was addressed to Corporal Bruce Gordon, Nineteenth Police Precinct, Marsport. Trench kept his eyes on it, his face filled with suspicion and the vague fear most men had for Security.

"Yeah," he said again. "Okay, probably routine. Only next time, Gordon, put the *facts* on your record with the Force. If you're a deportee, it should show up. That's all!"

Bruce Gordon went out, holding the envelope. The warning in Trench's voice wasn't for any omission on his record, he knew. He shoved the envelope into his belt pocket and waited until he was in his own room before opening it.

It was terse, and unsigned.

Report expected, overdue. Failure to observe duty will result in permanent resettlement to Mercury.

He swore, coldly and methodically, while his stomach dug knots in itself. The damned, stupid, blundering fools! That was all Trench and the police gang had to see; it was obvious that the letter had been opened. Sure, report at once. Drop a letter in the mailbox, and the next morning it would be turned over to Commissioner Arliss' office. Report or be kicked off to a planet that Security felt enough worse than Mars to use as punishment! Report *and* find Mars a worse place than Mercury could ever be.

He felt sick as he stood up to find paper and pen and write a terse, factual account of his own personal doings—minus any hint of anything wrong with the system here. Security might think it was enough for the moment, and the local men might possibly decide it a mere required formality. At least it would stall things off for a while...

But Gordon knew now that he could never hope to get back to Earth legally. That vague promise by Security was so much hogwash; yet it was surprising how much he had counted on it.

He tore the envelope from Security into tiny shreds, too small for Mother Corey to make sense of, and went out to mail the letter, feeling the few bills in his pocket. As usual, less than a hundred credits.

He passed a sound truck blatting out a campaign speech by candidate Nolan, filled with too-obvious facts about the present administration, together with hints that Wayne had paid to have Nolan assassinated. Gordon saw a crowd around it and was surprised, until he recognized them as Rafters—men from the biggest of the gangs supporting Wayne. The few citizens on the street who drifted toward the truck took a good look at them and moved on hastily.

It seemed incredible that Wayne could be re-elected, though, even with the power of the gangs. Nolan was probably a grafter, too; but he'd at least be a change, and certainly the citizens were aching for that.

The next day his relief was later. Gordon waited, trying to swallow their petty punishments, but it went against the grain. Finally, he began making the rounds, acting as his own night man. The owners of the joints didn't care whether they paid the second daily dole to the same man or another, but they wouldn't pay it again that same night. He'd managed to tap most of the places before his relief showed. He made no comment, but dutifully filled out the proper portion of both takes for the Voluntary Donation box. It wouldn't do his record any good with Trench, but it should put an end to the overtime.

Trench, however, had other ideas. The overtime continued, but it was dull after that—which made it even more tiring. But the time he took a special release out to the spaceport was the worst. Seeing the big ship readying for take-off back to Earth...

Then it was the day before election. The street was already bristling with barricades around the entrances, and everything ran with a last desperate restlessness, as if there would be no tomorrow. The operators all swore that Wayne would be elected, but seemed to fear a miracle. On the poorer section of the beat, there was a spiritless hope that Nolan might come in with his reform program. Men who would normally have been punctilious about their payments were avoiding Bruce Gordon, if in hope that, by putting it off a day or so, they could run into a period where no such payment would ever be asked—or a smaller one, at least. And he was too tired to chase them down. His collections had been falling off already, and he knew that he'd be on the carpet for that, if he didn't do better. It was a rich territory, and required careful mining; even as the week had gone, he still had more money in his wallet than he had expected.

But there had to be still more before night.

He was lucky; he came on a pusher working one of the better houses—long after his collections should have been over. He knew by the man's face that no protection had been paid higher up. The pusher was well-heeled; Gordon confiscated the money.

This time, Izzy made no protest. Lifting the roll of anyone outside the enforced part of Mars' laws was apparently honest, in his eyes. He nodded, and pointed to the man's belt. "Pick up the snow, too."

The pusher's face paled. He must have had his total capital with him, because stark ruin shone in his eyes. "Good God, Sergeant," he pleaded, "leave me something! I'll make it right. I'll cut you in. I gotta have some of that for myself!"

Gordon grimaced. He couldn't work up any great sympathy for anyone who made a living out of drugs.

They cleaned the pusher, and left him sitting on the steps, a picture of slumped misery. Izzy nodded approval. "Let him feel it a while. No sense jailing him yet. Bloody fool had no business starting without lining the groove. Anyhow, we'll get a bunch of credits for the stuff when we turn it in."

"Credits?" Gordon asked.

"Sure." Izzy patted the little package. "We get a quarter value. Captain probably gets fifty per cent from one of the pushers who's lined with him. Everybody's happy."

"Why not push it ourselves?" Gordon asked in disgust.

"Wouldn't be honest, gov'nor. Cops are supposed to turn it in."

Trench was almost jovial when he weighed the package and examined it to find how much it had been cut. He issued them slips, which they added as part of the contributions. "Good work—you, too, Gordon. Best week in the territory for a couple of months. I guess the citizens like you, the way they treat you." He laughed at his stale joke, and Gordon was willing to laugh with him. The credit on the dope had paid for most of the contributions. For once, he had money to show for the week.

Then Trench motioned Bruce Gordon forward, and dismissed Izzy with a nod of his head. "Something to discuss, Gordon. Isaacs, we're holding a little meeting, so wait around.

You're a sergeant already. But, Gordon, I'm offering you a chance. There aren't enough openings for all the good men, but... Oh, bother the soft soap. We're still short on election funds, so there's a raffle. The two men holding winning tickets get bucked up to sergeants. A hundred credits a ticket. How many?"

He frowned as Gordon counted out three bills. "You have a better chance with more tickets. A *much* better chance!"

The hint was hardly veiled. Gordon stuck the tickets into his wallet. Mars was a fine planet for picking up easy money—but holding it was another matter.

Trench counted the money and put it away. "Thanks, Gordon. That fills *my* quota. Look, you've been on overtime all week. Why not skip the meeting? Isaacs can brief you, later. Go out and get drunk, or something."

The comparative friendliness of the peace offering was probably the ultimate in graciousness from Trench. Idly, Gordon wondered what kind of pressures the captains were under; it must be pretty stiff, judging by the relief the man was showing at making quota.

"Thanks," he said, but his voice was bitter in his ears. "I'll go home and rest. Drinking costs too much for what I make. It's a good thing you don't have income tax here."

"We do," Trench said flatly; "forty per cent. Better make out a form next week, and start paying it regularly. But you can deduct your contributions here."

Gordon got out before he learned more good news.

CHAPTER SEVEN
Electioneering

As Bruce Gordon came out from the precinct house, he noticed the sounds first. Under the huge dome that enclosed the main part of the city, the heavier air pressure permitted normal travel of sound; and he'd become sensitive to the voice of the city after the relative quiet of the Nineteenth Precinct. But now the normal noise was different. There was an undertone of hushed waiting, with the sharp bursts of hammering and last-minute work standing out sharply through it. Voting booths were being finished here and there, and at one a small truck was delivering ballots. Voting by machine had never been established here. Wherever the booths were being thrown up, the nearby establishments were rushing gates and barricades in front of the buildings.

Most of the shops were already closed—even some of the saloons. To make up for it, stands were being placed along the streets, carrying banners that proclaimed free beer for all loyal administration friends. The few bars that were still open had been blessed with the sign of some mob, and obviously were well staffed with hoodlums ready to protect the proprietor. Private houses were boarded up. The scattering of last-minute shoppers along the streets showed that most of the citizens were laying in supplies to last until after election.

Gordon passed the First Marsport Bank and saw that it was surrounded by barbed wires, with other strands still being strung, and with a sign proclaiming that there was high voltage in the wires. Watching the operation was Jurgens; it was obvious that his hoodlums had been hired for the job.

Toward the edge of the dome, where Mother Corey's place was, the narrower streets were filling with the gangs, already half-drunk and marching about with their banners and printed signs. Curiously enough, all the gangs weren't working for Wayne's re-election. The big Star Point gang had apparently grown tired of the increasing cost of protection from the government, and was actively campaigning for Nolan. Their home territory reached nearly to Mother Corey's, before it ran into the no man's land separating it from the gang of Nick the Croop. The Croopsters were loyal to Wayne.

Gordon turned into his usual short-cut, past a rambling plastics plant and through the yard where their trucks were parked. He had half expected to find it barricaded, but apparently the rumors that Nick the Croop owned it were true; it would be protected in other ways, with the trucks used for street fighting, if needed. He threaded his way between two of the trucks.

Then a yell reached his ears, and something swished at him. An egg-sized rock hit the truck behind him and bounced back, just as he spotted a hoodlum drawing back a sling for a second shot.

Gordon was on his knees between heartbeats, darting under one of the trucks. He rolled to his feet, letting out a yell of his own, and plunged forward. His fist hit the thug in the elbow, just as the man's hand reached for his knife. His other hand chopped around, and the edge of his palm connected with the other's nose. Cartilage crunched, and a shrill cry of agony lanced out.

But the hoodlum wasn't alone. Another came out from the rear of one of the trucks. Gordon ducked as a knife sailed for his head; they were stupid enough not to aim for his stomach, at least. He bent down to locate some of the rubble on the ground, cursing his folly in carrying his knife under his uniform. The new beat had given him a false sense of security.

He found a couple of rocks and a bottle and let them fly, then bent for more.

Something landed on his back, and fingernails were gouging into his face, searching for his eyes!

Instinct carried him forward, jerking down sharply and twisting. The figure on his back sailed over his head, to land with a harsh thump on the ground. Brassy yellow hair spilled over a girl's face, and her breath slammed out of her throat as she hit. But the fall hadn't been enough to do serious damage.

Bruce Gordon jumped forward, bringing his foot up in a savage swing, but she'd rolled, and the blow only glanced against her ribs. She jerked her hand down for a knife, and came to her knees, her lips drawn back against her teeth. "Get him!" she yelled. Then he recognized her—Sheila Corey.

The two thugs had held back, but now they began edging in. Gordon slipped back behind another truck, listening for the sound of their feet. He'd half-expected another encounter with the Mother's granddaughter.

They tried to outmaneuver him; he stepped back to his former spot, catching his breath and digging frantically for his knife. It came out, just as they realized he'd tricked them.

Sheila was still on her knees, fumbling with something, and apparently paying no attention to him. But now she jerked to her feet, her hand going back and forward.

It was a six-inch section of pipe, with a thin wisp of smoke, and the throw was toward Gordon's feet. The hoodlums yelled, and ducked, while Sheila broke into a run away from him. The little homemade bomb landed, bounced, and lay still, with its fuse almost burned down.

Gordon's heart froze in his throat, but he was already in action. He spat savagely into his hand, and jumped for the bomb. If the fuse was powder-soaked, he had no chance. He brought his palm down against it, and heard a faint hissing. Then he held his breath, waiting.

No explosion came. It had been a crude job, with only a wick for a fuse.

Sheila Corey had stopped at a safe distance; now she grabbed at her helpers, and swung them with her. The three came back, Sheila in the lead with her knife flashing.

Gordon side-stepped her rush, and met the other two head-on, his knife swinging back. His foot hit some of the rubble on the ground at the last second, and he skidded. The leading mobster saw the chance and jumped for him. Gordon bent his head sharply, and dropped, falling onto his shoulders and somersaulting over. He twisted at the last second, jerking his arms down to come up facing the other.

Then a new voice cut into the fracas, and there was the sound of something landing against a skull with a hollow thud. Gordon got his head up just in time to see a man in police uniform kick aside the first hoodlum and lunge for the other. There was a confused flurry; then the second went up into the air and came down in the newcomer's hands, to land with a sickening jar and lie still. Behind, Sheila Corey lay crumpled in a heap, clutching one wrist in the other hand and crying silently.

Bruce Gordon came to his feet and started for her. She saw him coming, cast a single glance at the knife that had been knocked from her hands, then sprang aside and darted back through the parked trucks. In the street, she could lose herself in the swarm of Nick's Croopsters; Gordon turned back.

The iron-gray hair caught his eyes first. Then, as the solidly built figure turned, he grunted. It was Captain Murdoch—now dressed in the uniform of a regular beat cop, without even a corporal's stripes. And the face was filled with lines of strain that hadn't been there before.

Murdoch threw the second gangster up into a truck after the first one and slammed the door shut, locking it with the metal bar which had apparently been his weapon. Then he grinned wryly, and came back toward Gordon.

"You seem to have friends here," he commented. "A good thing I was trying to catch up with you. Just missed you at the Precinct House, came after you, and saw you turn in here. Then I heard the rumpus. A good thing for me, too, maybe."

Gordon blinked, accepting the other's hand. "How so? And what happened?" He indicated the bare sleeve.

"One's the result of the other," Murdoch told him. "They've got me sewed up, and they're throwing the book at me. The old laws make me a citizen while I wear the uniform—and a citizen can't quit the Force. That puts me out of Earth's jurisdiction. I can't even cable for funds, and I guess I'm too old to start squeezing money out of citizens. I was coming to ask whether you had room in your diggings for a guest—and I'm hoping now that my part here cinches it."

Murdoch had tried to treat it lightly, but Gordon saw the red creeping up into the man's face. "Forget that part. There's room enough for two in my place—and I guess Mother Corey won't mind. I'm damned glad you were following me."

"So'm I, Gordon. What'll we do with the prisoners?"

"Leave 'em; we couldn't get a Croopster locked up tonight for anything."

He started ahead, leading the way through the remaining trucks and back to the street that led to Mother Corey's. Murdoch fell in step with him. "This is the first time I've had to look you up," he said. "I've been going out nights to help the citizens organize against the Stonewall gang. But that's over now—they gave me hell for inciting vigilante action, and confined me inside the dome. The way they hate a decent cop here, you'd think honesty was contagious."

"Yeah." Gordon preferred to let it drop. Murdoch was being given the business for going too far on the Stonewall gang, not for refusing to take normal graft.

They came to the gray three-story building that Mother Corey now owned. Gordon stopped, realizing for the first time that there was no trace of efforts to protect it against the coming night and day. The entrance was unprotected. Then his eyes caught the bright chalk marks around it—notices to the gangs to keep hands off. Mother Corey evidently had pull enough to get every mob in the neighborhood to affix its seal.

As he drew near, though, two men edged across the street from a clump watching the beginning excitement. Then, as they identified Gordon, they moved back again. Some of the

Mother's old lodgers from the ruin outside the dome were inside now—obviously posted where it would do the most good.

Corey stuck his head out of the door at the back of the hall as Gordon entered, and started to retire again—until he spotted Murdoch. Gordon explained the situation hastily.

"It's your room, cobber," the old man wheezed. He waddled back, to come out with a towel and key, which he handed to Murdoch. "Number forty-two."

His heavy hand rested on Gordon's arm, holding the younger man back. Murdoch gave Gordon a brief, tired smile, and started for the stairs. "Thanks, Gordon. I'm turning in right now."

Mother Corey shook his head, shaking the few hairs on his head and face, and the wrinkles in his doughy skin deepened. "Hasn't changed, that one. Must be thirty years, but I'd know Asa Murdoch anywhere. Took me to the spaceport, handed me my yellow ticket, and sent me off for Mars. A nice, clean kid—just like my own boy was. But Murdoch wasn't like the rest of the neighborhood. He still called me 'sir,' when my boy was walking across the street, so the lad wouldn't know they were sending me away. Oh well, that was a long time ago, cobber. A long time."

He rubbed a pasty hand over his chin, shaking his head and wheezing heavily. Gordon chuckled. "Well, how—?"

Something banged heavily against the entrance seal, and there was the sound of a hot argument, followed by a commotion of some sort. Corey seemed to prick up his ears, and began to waddle rapidly toward the entrance.

It broke open before he could reach it, the seal snapping back to show a giant of a man outside holding the two guards from across the street, while a scar-faced, dark man shoved through briskly. Corey snapped out a quick word, and the two guards ceased struggling and started back across the street. The giant pushed in after the smaller thug.

"I'm from the Ajax Householders Protection Group," the dark man announced officially. "We're selling election protection. And brother, do you need it, if you're counting on those mugs. We're assessing you—"

"Not long on Mars, are you?" Mother Corey asked. The whine was entirely missing from his voice now, though his face seemed as expressionless as ever. "What does your boss Jurgens figure on doing, punk? Taking over *all* the rackets for the whole city?"

The dark face snarled, while the giant moved a step forward. Then he shrugged. "Okay, Fatty. So Jurgens is behind it. So now you know. And I'm doubling your assessment, right now. To you, it's—"

A heavy hand fell on the man's shoulder, and Mother Corey leaned forward slightly. Even in Mars' gravity, his bulk made the other buckle at the knees. The hand that had been reaching for the knife yanked the weapon out and brought it up sharply.

Gordon started to step in, then, but there was no time. Mother Corey's free hand came around in an open-palmed slap that lifted the collector up from the floor and sent him reeling back against a wall. The knife fell from the crook's hand, and the dark face turned pale. He sagged down the wall, limply.

The giant opened his mouth, and took half a step forward; but the only sound he made was a choking gobble. Mother Corey moved without seeming haste, but before the other could make up his mind. There was a series of motions that seemed to have no pattern. The giant was spun around, somehow; one arm was jerked back behind him, then the other was forced up to it. Mother Corey held the wrists in one hand, put his other under the giant's crotch, and lifted.

Carrying the big figure off the floor, the old man moved toward the seal. His foot found the button, snapping the entrance open. He pitched the giant out overhanded; holding the entrance, he reached for the dark man with one hand and tossed him on top of the giant.

"To me, it's nothing," he called out. "Take these two back to young Jurgens, boys, and tell him to keep his punks out of my house."

The entrance snapped shut then, and Corey turned back to Gordon, wiping the wisps of hair from his face. He was still wheezing asthmatically, but there seemed to be no change in the rhythm of his breathing. "As I was going to say, cobber," he said, "we've got a little social game going upstairs—the room with the window. Fine view of the parades. We need a fourth."

Gordon started to protest that he was tired and needed his sleep; then he shrugged. Corey's house was one of the few that had kept some relation to Earth styles by installing a couple of windows in the second story, and it would give a perfect view of the street. He followed the old man up the stairs.

Two other men were already in the surprisingly well-furnished room, at the little table set up near the window. Bruce Gordon recognized one as Randolph, the publisher of the little opposition paper. The man's pale blondness, weak eyes, and generally rabbity expression totally belied the courage that had permitted him to keep going at his hopeless task of trying to clean up Marsport. The *Crusader* was strictly a one-man weekly, against Mayor Wayne's *Chronicle*, with its Earth-comics and daily circulation of over a hundred thousand. Wayne apparently let the paper stay in business to give himself a talking point about fair play; but Randolph walked with a limp from the last working over he had received.

"Hi, Gordon," he said. His thin, high voice was cool and reserved, in keeping with the opinion he had expressed publicly of the police as a body. But he did not protest Corey's selection of a partner. "This is Ed Praeger. He's an engineer on our railroad."

Gordon acknowledged the introduction automatically. He'd almost forgotten that Marsport was the center of a thinly populated area, stretching for a thousand miles in all directions beyond the city, connected by the winding link of the electric monorail. "So there really is a surrounding countryside," he said.

Praeger nodded. He was a big, open-faced man, just turning bald. His handshake was firm and friendly. "There are even cities out there, Gordon. Nothing like Marsport, but that's no loss. That's where the real population of Mars is—decent people, men who are going to turn this into a real planet some day."

"There are plenty like that here, too," Randolph said. He picked up the cards. "First ace deals. Damn it, Mother, sit down-wind from me, won't you? Or else take a bath."

Mother Corey chuckled, and wheezed his way up out of the chair, exchanging places with Gordon. "I got a surprise for you, cobber," he said, and there was only amusement in his voice. "I got me in fifty gallons of water today, and tomorrow I do just that. Made up my mind there was going to be a cleanup in Marsport, even if Wayne does win. And stop examining the cards, Bruce. I don't cheat my friends. The readers are put away for old-times' sake."

Randolph shrugged, and went on as if he hadn't interrupted himself. "Ninety per cent of Marsport is decent. They have to be. It takes at least nine honest men to support a crook. They come up here to start over—maybe spent half their life saving up for the trip. They hear a man can make fifty credits a day in the factories, or strike it rich crop prospecting. What they don't realize is that things cost ten times as much here, too. They plan, maybe, on getting rich and going back to Earth…"

"Nobody goes back," Mother Corey wheezed. *'I* know." His eyes rested on Gordon.

"A lot don't want to," Praeger said. "I never meant to go back. I've got me a farm up north. Another ten years, and I retire to it. My kids are up there now—grandkids, that is. They're Martians; maybe you won't believe me, but they can breathe the air here without a helmet."

The others nodded. Gordon had learned that a fair number of third-generation people got that way. Their chests were only a trifle larger, and their heartbeat only a few points higher; it was an internal adaptation, like the one that had occurred in test animals reared at a simulated forty-thousand-feet altitude on Earth, before Mars was ever settled.

"They'll take the planet away from Earth yet," Randolph agreed. "Marsport is strictly artificial. It's kept going only because it's the only place where Earth will set down her ships. If Security doesn't do anything, time will."

"Security!" Gordon muttered bitterly. Security was good at getting people in trouble, but he had seen no other sign of it.

Randolph frowned over his cards. "Yeah, I know. The government set them up, gave them a mixture of powers, and has been trying to keep them from working ever since. But somehow they did clean up Venus; and every crook here is scared to death of the name. How come a muckraking newspaperman like you never turned up anything on them, Gordon?"

Gordon shrugged. It was the first reference he'd heard to his background, and he preferred to let it drop.

But Mother Corey cut in, his voice older and hoarser, and the skin on his jowls even grayer than usual. "Don't sell them short, cobber. I did…once… You forget them, here, after a while. But they're around…"

Bruce Gordon felt something run down his armpit, and a chill creep up his back...

Out on the street, a sudden whooping began, and he glanced down. The parade was on, the Croopsters in full swing, already mostly drunk. The main body went down the street, waving fluorescent signs, while side-guards preceded them, armed with axes, knocking aside the flimsier barricades as they went. He watched a group break into a small grocery store to come out with bundles. They dragged out the storekeeper, his wife, and young daughter, and pressed them into the middle of the parade.

"If Security's so damned powerful, why doesn't it stop that?" he asked bitterly.

Randolph grinned at him. "They might do it, Gordon. They just might. But are you sure you want it stopped?"

"All right," Mother Corey said suddenly. "This is a social game, cobbers."

Outside, the parade picked up enthusiasm as smaller gangs joined behind the main one. There were a fair number of plain citizens who had been impressed into it, too, judging by the appearance of little frightened groups in the middle of the mobsters.

Gordon couldn't understand why the police hadn't at least been kept on duty, until Honest Izzy came into the room. The little man found a chair and bought chips silently; he looked tired.

"Vacation?" Mother Corey asked.

Izzy nodded. "Trench took forever giving it to us, Mother. But it's the same old deal; all the police gees get tomorrow off—you, too, gov'nor. No cops to influence the vote, that's the word. We even gotta wear civvies when we go out to vote for Wayne."

Gordon looked down at the rioters, who were now only keeping up a pretense of a parade. It would be worse tomorrow, he supposed; and there would be no cops. The image of the old woman and her husband in the little liquor store where he'd had his first experience came back to him. He wondered how well barricaded they were.

He felt the curious eyes of Mother Corey dancing from him to Izzy and back, and heard the old man's chuckle. "Put a uniform on some men and they begin to believe they're cops, eh, cobber?"

He shoved up from the table abruptly and headed for his room, swearing to himself.

CHAPTER EIGHT
Vote Early and Often

Izzy was up first the next morning, urging them to hurry before things began to hum. From somewhere, he dug up a suit of clothes that Murdoch could wear. He found the gun that Gordon had confiscated from O'Neill and filled it from a box of ammunition he'd apparently purchased.

"I picked up some special permits," he said. "I knew you had this cannon, gov'nor, and I figured it'd come in handy. Wouldn't be caught dead with one myself. Knives, that's my specialty. Come on, Cap'n, we gotta get out the vote."

Murdoch shook his head. "In the first place, I'm not registered."

Izzy grinned. "Every cop's registered in his own precinct; Wayne got the honor system fixed for us. Show your papers and go into any booth in your territory. That's all. And you'd better be seen voting often, too, Cap'n. What's your precinct?"

"Eleventh, but I'm not voting. I'd like to come along with you to observe, but I wouldn't make any choice between Wayne and Nolan."

Downstairs, the rear room was locked, with one of Mother Corey's guards at the door. From inside came the rare sound of water splashing, mixed with a wheezing, off-key caterwauling. Mother Corey was apparently making good on his promise to take a bath. As they reached the hall, one of Trench's lieutenants came through the entrance, waving his badge at the protesting man outside.

He spotted the three, and jerked his thumb. "Come on, you. We're late. And I ain't staying on the streets when it gets going."

A small police car was waiting outside, and they headed for it. Bruce Gordon looked at the debacle left behind the drunken, looting mob. Most of the barricades were down. Here and there, a few citizens were rushing about trying to restore them, keeping wary eyes on the mobsters who had passed out on the streets.

Suddenly a siren blasted out in sharp bursts, and the lieutenant jumped. "Come on, you gees. I gotta be back in half an hour."

They piled inside, and the little electric car took off at its top speed. But now the quietness had been broken. There were trucks coming out of the plastics plant, and mobsters were gathering up their drunks, and chasing the citizens back into their houses. Some of them were wearing the forbidden guns, but it wouldn't matter on a day when no police were on duty.

In the Ninth Precinct, the Planters were the biggest gang, and all the others were temporarily enrolled under them. Here, there were less signs of trouble. The joints had been better barricaded, and the looting had been kept to a minimum.

The three got off. A scooter pulled up alongside them almost at once, with a gun-carrying mobster riding it. "You mugs get the hell out of—Oh, cops! Okay, better pin these on."

He handed out gaudy arm bands, and the three fastened them in place. Nearly everyone else already had them showing. The Planters were moving efficiently. They were grouped around the booths, and they had begun to line up their men, putting them in position to begin voting at once.

Then the siren hooted again, a long, steady blast. The bunting in front of the booths was pulled off, and the lines began to move. Izzy led the way to the one at the rich end of their beat, and moved toward the head of the line. "Cops," he said to the six mobsters who surrounded the booth. "We got territory to cover."

A thumb indicated that they could go in. Murdoch remained outside, and one of the thugs reached for him. Izzy cut him off. "Just a friend on the way to his own route. Eleventh Precinct."

There were scowls, but they let it go. Then Gordon was in the little booth. It seemed to be in order. There were the books of registration, with a checker for Wayne, one for Nolan, and a third, supposedly neutral, behind the plank that served as a desk. The Nolan man was protesting.

"He's been dead for ten years. I know him. He's my uncle."

"There's a Mike Thaler registered, and this guy says he's Thaler," the Wayne man said decisively. "He votes."

One of the Planters passed his gun to the inspector for the Wayne side. The Nolan man gulped, and nodded. "Heh-heh, yes, just a mix-up. He's registered, so he votes."

The next man Gordon recognized as being from one of the small shops on his beat. The fellow's eyes were desperate, but he was forcing himself to go through with it. "Murtagh," he said, and his voice broke on the second syllable. "Owen Murtagh."

"Murtang... No registration!" The Wayne checker shrugged. "Next!"

"It's Murtagh. M-U-R-T-A-G-H. Owen Murtagh, of 738 Morrisy—"

"Protest!" The Wayne man cut off the frantic wriggling of the Nolan checker's finger toward the line in the book. "When a man can't get the name straight the first time, it's suspicious."

The supposedly neutral checker nodded. "Better check the name off, unless the real Murtagh shows up. Any objections, Yeoman?"

The Nolan man had no objections—outwardly. He was sweating, and the surprise in his eyes indicated that this was all new to him.

Bruce Gordon came next, showing his badge. He was passed with a nod, and headed for the little closed-off polling place. But the Wayne man touched his arm and indicated a ballot. There were two piles, and this pile was already filled out for Wayne. "Saves trouble, unless you want to do it yourself," he suggested.

Gordon shrugged, and shoved it into the slot. He went outside and waited for Izzy to follow. It was raw beyond anything he'd expected—but at least it saved any doubt about the votes.

The procedure was the same at the next booth, though they had more trouble. The Nolan man there was a fool—neither green nor agreeable. He protested vigorously, in spite of a suspicious bruise along his temple, and finally made some of the protests stick.

Gordon began to wonder how it could be anything but a clear unanimous vote, at that rate. Izzy shook his head. "Wayne'll win, but not that easy. The sticks don't have strong mobs, and they'll pile up a heavy Nolan vote. And you'll see things hum soon!"

Gordon had voted three times under the "honor system," before he saw. They were just nearing a polling place when a heavy truck came careening around a corner. Men began piling out of the back before it stopped—men armed with clubs and stones. They were in the middle of the Planters at once, striking without science, but with ferocity. The line waiting to vote broke up, but the citizens had apparently organized with care. A good number of the men in the line were with the attackers.

There was the sound of a shot, and a horrified cry. For a second, the citizens broke; then a wave of fury seemed to wash over them at the needless risk to the safety of all. The horror of rupturing the dome was strongly ingrained in every citizen of Marsport. They drew back, then made a concerted rush. There was a trample of bodies, but no more shots.

In a minute, the citizens' group was inside, ripping the fixed ballots to shreds, filling out and dropping their own. They ignored the registration clerks.

A whistle had been shrilling for minutes. Now another group came onto the scene, and the Planters' men began getting out rapidly. Some of the citizens looked up and yelled, but it was too late. From the approaching cars, pipes projected forward. Streams of liquid jetted out, and their agonized cries followed.

Even where he stood, Gordon could smell the fumes of ammonia. Izzy's face tensed, and he swore. "Inside the dome! They're poisoning the air."

But the trick worked. In no time, men in crude masks were clearing out the booth, driving the last struggling citizens away, and getting ready for business as usual.

Murdoch turned on his heel. "I've had enough. I've made up my mind," he said. "The cable offices must be open for the doctored reports on the election to Earth. Where's the nearest?"

Izzy frowned, but supplied the information. Bruce Gordon pulled Murdoch aside. "Come off the head-cop role; it won't work. They must have had reports on elections before this."

"Damn the trouble. It's never been this raw before. Look at Izzy's face, Gordon. Even he's shocked. Something has to be done about this, before worse happens. I've still got connections back there—"

"Okay," Gordon said bitterly. He'd liked Asa Murdoch, had begun to respect him. It hurt to see that what he'd considered hardheadedness was just another case of a fool fighting dragons with a paper sword.

"Okay, it's your death certificate," he said, and turned back toward Izzy. "Go send your sob stories, Murdoch."

They taught a bunch of pretty maxims in school—even slum kids learned that honesty was the best policy, while their honest parents rotted in unheated holes, and the racketeers rode around in fancy cars. It had got him once. He'd refused to take a dive as a boxer; he'd tried to play honest cards; he'd tried honesty on his beat back on Earth. He'd tried to help the suckers in his column, and here he was.

And Gordon had been proud to serve under Murdoch.

"Come on, Izzy," he said. "Let's vote!"

Izzy shook his head. "It ain't right, gov'nor."

"Let him do what he damn pleases," Gordon told him.

Izzy's small face puckered up in lines of worry. "No, I don't mean him. I mean this business of using ammonia. I know some of the gees trying to vote. They been paying me off—and that's a retainer, you might say. Now this gang tries to poison them. I'm still running an honest beat, and I bloody well can't vote for that! Uniform or no uniform, I'm walking beat today. And the first gee that gives trouble to the men who pay me gets a knife where he eats. When I get paid for a job, I do the job."

Gordon watched him head down the block, and started after the little man. Then he grimaced. Rule books! Even Izzy had one.

He went down the row, voting regularly. The Planters had things in order. The mess had already been cleaned up when he arrived at the cheaper end of the beat. It was the last place where he'd be expected to do his duty by Wayne's administration; he waited in line.

Then a voice hit at his ears, and he looked up to see Sheila Corey only two places in front of him. "Mrs. Mary Edelstein," she was saying. The Wayne man nodded, and there was no protest. She picked up a Wayne ballot, and dropped it in the box.

Then her eyes fell on Gordon. She hesitated for a second, bit her lips, and finally moved out into the crowd.

He could see no sign of her as he stepped out a minute later, but the back of his neck prickled.

He started out of the crowd, trying to act normal, but glancing down to make sure the gun was in its proper position. Satisfied, he wheeled suddenly and spotted her behind him, before she could slip out of sight.

Then a shout went up, yanking his eyes around with the rest of those standing near. The eyes had centered on the alleys along the street, and men were beginning to run wildly, while others were jerking out their weapons. He saw a big gray car coming up the street; on its side was painted the colors of the Planters. Now it swerved, hitting a siren button.

But it was too late. Trucks shot out of the little alleys, jamming forward through the people; there must have been fifty of them. One hit the big gray car, tossing it aside. It was Trench himself who leaped out, together with the driver. The trucks paid no attention, but bore down on the crowd. From one of them, a machine gun opened fire.

Gordon dropped and began crawling in the only direction that was open, straight toward the alleys from which the trucks had come. A few others had tried that, but most were darting back as they saw the colors of Nolan's Star Point gang on the trucks.

Other guns began firing; men were leaping from the trucks and pouring into the mob of Planters, forcing their way toward the booth in the center of the mess.

It was a beautifully timed surprise attack, and a well-armed one, even though guns were supposed to be so rare here. Gordon stumbled into someone ahead of him, and saw it was Trench. He looked up, and straight into the swinging muzzle of the machine gun that had started the commotion.

Trench was reaching for his revolver, but he was going to be too late. Gordon brought his up the extra half inch, aiming by the feel, and pulled the trigger. The man behind the machine gun dropped.

Trench had his gun out now, and was firing, after a single surprised glance at Gordon. He waved back toward the crowd.

But Gordon had spotted the open trunk of the gray car. He shook his head and tried to indicate it. Trench jerked his thumb and leaped to his feet, rushing back.

Gordon saw another truck go by, and felt a bullet miss him by inches. Then his legs were under him, and he was sliding into the big luggage compartment, where the metal would shield him.

Something soft under his feet threw him down. He felt a body under him, and coldness washed over him before he could get his eyes down. The cold went away, to be replaced by shock. Between his spread knees lay Murdoch, bound and gagged, his face a bloody mess.

Gordon reached for the gag, but the other held up his hands and pointed to the gun. It made sense. The knots were tight, but Gordon managed to get his knife under the rope around Murdoch's wrists and slice through it. The older man's hands went out for the gun; his eyes swung toward the street, while Gordon attacked the rope around his ankles.

The Star Point men were winning, though it was tough going. They had fought their way almost to the booth, but there a V of Planters' cars had been gotten into position somehow, and gunfire was coming from behind them. As he watched, a huge man reached over one of the cars, picked up a Star Point man, and lifted him behind the barricade.

The gag had just come out when the Star Point man jumped into view again, waving a rag over his head and yelling. Captain Trench followed him out, and began pointing toward the gray car.

"They want me," Murdoch gasped thickly. "Get out, Gordon, before they gang up on us!"

Gordon jerked his eyes back toward the alley on the other side. It went at an angle and would offer some protection.

He looked back, just as bullets began to land against the metal of the car. Murdoch held up one finger and put himself into a position to make a run for it. Then he brought the finger down sharply, and the two leaped out.

Trench's ex-Marine bellow carried over the fighting. "Get the old man!"

Bruce Gordon had no time to look back. He hit the alley in five heart-ripping leaps and was around the bend. Then he swung, just as Murdoch made it. Bullets spatted against the walls, and he saw blood pumping from under Murdoch's right shoulder.

"Keep going!" Murdoch ordered.

A fresh cry from the street cut into his order, however. Gordon risked a quick look, then stepped farther out to make sure.

The surprise raid by the Star Pointers hadn't been quite as much of a surprise as expected. Coming down the street, with no regard for men trying to get out of their way, the trucks of the Croopsters were battering aside the few who could not reach safety. There were no machine guns this time.

They smacked into the tangle of Star Point trucks, and came to a grinding halt, men piling out ready for battle. Gordon nodded. In a few minutes, Wayne's supporters would have the booth again; there'd be a delay before any organized search could be made for the fugitives. He looked down at Murdoch's shoulder.

"Come on," he said finally. "Or should I carry you?"

Murdoch shook his head. "I'll walk. Get me to a place where we can talk—and be damned to this. Gordon, I've got to talk—but I don't have to live. I mean that!"

Gordon started off, disregarding the words; a place of safety had to come first. He picked his way down alleys and small streets. The older man kept trying to stop to speak, but Gordon gave him no opportunity. There was one chance...

It was farther than he'd thought, and Gordon began to suspect he'd missed the way, until he saw the drugstore. Now it all fell into place—the first beat he'd had with Izzy.

He ducked down back alleys until he reached the right section. He scanned the street, jumped to the door of the little liquor store and began banging on it. There was no answer, though he was sure the old couple lived just over the store.

He began banging again. Finally, a feeble voice sounded from inside. "Who is it?"

"A man in distress!" he yelled back. There was no way to identify himself; he could only hope she would look.

The entrance seal opened briefly; then it flashed open all the way. He motioned to Murdoch, and jumped to help the failing man to the entrance. The old lady looked, then moved quickly to the other side.

"Ach, Gott," she breathed. Her hands trembled as she relocked the seal. Then she brushed the thin hair off her face, and pointed. Gordon followed her up the stairs, carrying Murdoch on his back. She opened a door, passed through a tiny kitchen, and threw open another door to a bedroom.

The old man lay on the bed, and this time there was no question of concussion. The woman nodded. "Yes. Pappa is dead, God forbid it. He *would* try to vote. I told him and told him—and then... With my own hands, I carried him here."

Gordon felt sick. He started to turn, but she shook her head quickly. "No. Pappa is dead. He needs no beds now, and your friend is suffering; put him here."

She lifted the frail body of the old man and lowered him onto the floor with a strength that seemed impossible. Then her hands were gentle as she helped lower Murdoch where the corpse had been. "I'll get alcohol from below—and bandages and hot water."

Asa Murdoch opened his eyes, breathing stertoriously. His face was blanched, his clothes a mess. But he protested as Gordon tried to strip them. "Let them go, kid. There's no way to save me now. And listen!"

"I'm listening!"

"With your *mind*, Gordon, not your ears. You've heard a lot about Security. Well, I'm Security. Top level—policy for Mars. We never got a top man here without his being discovered and killed—That's why we've had to work under all the cover—and against our own government. Nobody knew I was here—Trench was our man—Sold us out! We've got junior men—down to your level, clerks, such things. We've got a dozen plans. But we're not ready for an emergency, and it's here—now!

"Gordon, you're a self-made louse, but underneath it you're a man. That's why we rate you higher than you think. That's why I'm going to trust you—because I have to."

He swallowed, and the thin hand of the woman lifted brandy to his lips. "Pappa," she said slowly. "He was a clerk once for Security. But nobody came, nobody called…"

She went back to trying to bandage the bleeding bluish hole in his chest. Murdoch nodded faintly.

"Probably what happened to a lot—men like Trench, supposed to build an organization, just leaving the loose ends hanging." He groaned; sweat appeared on his forehead, but his eyes never left Gordon's. "Hell's going to pop. The government's waiting to step in; Earth *wants* to take over."

"It should," Gordon said.

"No! We've studied these things. Mars won't give up—and Earth wants a plum, not responsibility. You'll have civil war and the whole planetary development ruined. Security's the only hope, Gordon—the only chance Mars had, has, or will have! Believe me, I know. Security has to be notified. There's a code message I had ready—a message to a friend—even you can send it. And they'll be watching. I've got the basic plans in the book here."

He slumped back. Gordon frowned, then found the book and pulled it out as gently as he could. It was a small black memo book, covered with pages of shorthand. The back was an address book, filled with names—many crossed out. A sheet of paper in normal writing fell out.

"The message…" Murdoch took another swallow of brandy. "Take it. You're head of Security on Mars now. It's all authorized in the plans there. You'll need the brains and knowledge of the others—but they can't act. You can—we know about you."

The old woman sighed. She put down the hot water and picked up the bottle of brandy, starting down the stairs.

"Gordon!" Murdoch said faintly.

He turned to put his head down. From the stairs, a sudden cry and thump sounded, and something hit the floor. Gordon jumped toward the sound, to find the old lady bending over the inert figure of Sheila Corey.

"I heard someone," the woman said. She stared at the brandy bottle sickly. *"Gott in Himmel,* look at me. Am I a killer, too, that I should strike a young and beautiful girl. She comes into my house, and I sneak behind her... It is an evil time, young man. Here, you carry her inside. I'll get some twine to tie her up. The idea, spying on you!"

Gordon picked the girl up roughly. That capped it, he thought. There was no way of knowing how much she'd heard, or whether she'd tipped others off. He dropped her by the bed and went over to Murdoch, who was dying now.

"So Security wants me to contact the others in the book and organize things?"

"Yes." Murdoch swallowed. "Not a good chance, then—but a chance. Still time—I think. Gordon?"

"What else can I do?" Bruce Gordon asked.

He knew it was no answer, but Asa Murdoch apparently accepted it as a promise. The gray-speckled head relaxed and rolled sideways on the bloody pillow.

"Dead," Gordon said to the woman, as she came up with the twine. "Dead, fighting wind-mills. And maybe winning. I don't know."

He turned toward Sheila—a split second too late. The girl came up from the floor with a single push of her arm. She pivoted on her heel, hit the door, and her heels were clattering on the stairs. Before Gordon could reach the entrance, she was whipping around into an alley.

He watched her go, sick inside, and the last he saw was the hand she held up, waving the little black book at him!

He turned back into the liquor shop; the woman seemed to read his face. "I should have watched her. It is a bad day for me, young man. I failed Pappa; I failed the poor man who died—and now I have failed you. It is better..."

He caught her as she fell toward him. She relaxed after a second. "Upstairs, please," she whispered, "beside Pappa. There was nothing else. And these Martian poisons—they are so sure, they don't hurt. Five minutes more, I think. Stay with me, I'll tell you how Pappa and I got married. I want somebody should know how it was with us once, together."

He stayed, then picked the two bodies up and moved them from the floor onto the bed where he had first seen the old man. He moved Murdoch's body aside, and covered the two gently. Finally, he went down the stairs, carrying Murdoch with him. The man's weight was a stiff load, even on Mars; but, somehow, he couldn't leave his body with the old couple.

He stopped finally ten blocks of narrow alleys away, and put Murdoch down.

Now he had no witnesses, except Sheila Corey. He had no book, no clues as to whom to see and what to do.

He heard the sound of a mobile amplifier, and strained his ears toward it. He got enough to know that Wayne had won a thumping victory, better than three to two.

Isaiah Trench was still captain of the Seventh Precinct.

CHAPTER NINE
Contraband

Elections were over, but the few dim lights along the street showed only boarded-up and darkened buildings. There were sounds of stirring, but no one was trusting that the election-day brawls were completely ended yet.

Gordon hesitated, then swung glumly toward a corner where he could find a police call box. He heard a tiny patrol car turn the corner and ducked back into another alley to wait for it to go by. But they weren't looking for him. Their spotlight caught a running boy, clutching a few thin copies of the *Crusader* under a scrawny arm.

After the cops had dumped the unconscious kid into the back of the small squad car, and gone looking for more game, Gordon went over to look at the tattered scraps left of the opposition paper.

Randolph wasn't preaching this time, but was content to report the facts he'd seen. There had been at least ninety known killings; mobs had fought citizens outside the main market for three hours.

Yet in spite of all the ballot-stuffing and intimidations, Wayne had barely squeaked through, by a four per cent majority. It was obvious that the current administration could never win another election.

Bruce Gordon lifted the cradled phone from the box. "Gordon reporting," he announced.

A startled grunt came from the instrument, followed by the clicks of hasty switching. In less than fifteen seconds, Trench's voice barked out of the phone. "Gordon? Where the hell you been?"

"Up an alley between McCutcheon and Miles," Gordon told him. "With a corpse. Murdoch's corpse. Better send out the wagon."

Trench hesitated only a fraction of a second. "Okay, *I'll* be out in ten minutes."

Gordon clumped back to the alley and bent for a final inspection of Murdoch's body, to make sure nothing would prove the flaws in his weakly built story.

Isaiah Trench was better than his word. He swung his gray car up to the alley in seven minutes.

The door slammed behind him, a beam snapped out from his flashlight into the alley, and then he was beside Murdoch's body. He threw the light to Gordon and stooped to run expert hands over the corpse and through the pockets.

Finally, he stood up, frowning. "He's dead, all right. I don't get it. If you hadn't reported in… Gordon, did he try to make you think he was—"

"Security?" Gordon filled in. "Yeah. Claimed he was head of it here, and wanted me to send a message to Earth for him."

Trench nodded, a touch of relief on his face. "Crazy!"

Gordon grimaced faintly.

"Crazy," Trench repeated. "He must have been to spin that story… By the way, thanks for killing that sniper. You're a good shot. I'd be dead if you weren't, I guess."

Gordon made no comment, and Trench said, "I could start a nasty investigation, I guess. But I heard him raving, too. Give me a hand, and I'll take care of all this… Want me to drop you off?"

They wangled the body into the trunk of the car. Then it was good to relax while Trench drove along the rubble-piled and nearly deserted streets. Gordon heard a sigh from beside him; Trench must have been under tension, too.

They didn't speak until Trench stopped in front of Mother Corey's place. Then the captain turned and stuck out his hand. "Congratulations, by the way. I forgot to tell you, but you won the lottery. You're a sergeant from now on."

Inside, a thick effluvium hit his nose, and Gordon turned to see Mother Corey's huge bulk waddling down the hall. The old man nodded. "We thought you'd gone on the lam, cobber. But I guess, since Trench brought you back, you've cooled. Good, good. As a respectable man now, I couldn't have stashed you from the cops—though I might have been tempted—mighty tempted." His face was melancholy. "Tell me, lad, did they get Murdoch?"

Bruce Gordon nodded, and the old man sighed. Something suspiciously like a tear glistened in his eyes.

"I thought you were taking a bath," Gordon commented.

The old man chuckled. "Fate's against me, cobber. With all the shooting, some punk put a bullet clean through the wall and the plastic of the tub. Fifty gallons of water, all wasted!"

He turned back toward the end of the hall, sighing again. Gordon went up the stairs, noticing that Izzy's door was open. The little man was stretched out on the bunk in his clothes, filthy; one side of his face swollen.

"Hi, gov'nor," he called out, his voice still cheerful. "I had odds you'd beat the ticket, though the Mother and me were worried there for a while. How'd you grease the fix?"

Gordon sketched it in, without mentioning Security. "What happened to you, Izzy?"

"Price of being honest. But the gees who paid me protection didn't get hurt, gov'nor." He winced, then grinned. "So they pay double tomorrow. Honesty pays, gov'nor, if you squeeze it once in a while... Funny, you making sergeant; I thought two other gees won the lottery."

So the promotion *had* come from Trench! It bothered him. When a turkey sees corn on the menu, it's time to wonder about Thanksgiving.

Collections were good all week—probably as a result of Izzy's actions. Even after he arranged to pay his income tax, and turned over his "donation" to the fund, Gordon was well ahead for the first time since he'd landed here.

He had become almost superstitious about the way he was always left with no more than a hundred credits in his pockets. This time, he stripped himself to that sum at once, depositing the rest in the First Marsport Bank. Maybe it would break the jinx.

They were one of the few teams in the Seventh Precinct to make full quota. Trench was lavish in his praise. He was playing more than fair with Bruce Gordon now, but there was a basic suspicion in his eyes.

The next day, he drafted Izzy and Gordon for a trip outside the dome. "It's easy enough, and you'll get plenty of credit in the fund for it. I need two men who can keep their mouths shut."

They idled around the station through the morning. In the late afternoon, they left in a big truck capable of hauling what would have been fifty tons on Earth. Trench drove. Outside the dome, the electric motor carried them along at a steady twenty miles an hour, almost silently.

It was Gordon's first look at the real Mars. He saw small villages where crop prospectors and hydroponic farmers lived, with a few small industrial sections scattered over the desert. As they moved out, he saw the slow change from the beaten appearance of Marsport to something that seemed no worse than would be found among the share-croppers back on Earth. It was obvious that Marsport was the poison center here.

Some of the younger children were running around without helmets, confirming Praeger's claim that third-generation Martians somehow learned to adapt to the atmosphere.

Darkness fell sharply, as it always did in Mars' thin air, but they went on, heading out into the dunes of the desert. When they finally stopped, they were beside a small, battered space ship. Boxes were piled all around it, and others were being tossed out. Trent leaped from the truck, motioning them to follow, and they began loading the crates hastily. It took about an hour of hard work to load the last of them, and Trench was working harder than they were. Finished, he went up to one of the men from the ship, handed over an envelope, and came back to start the truck back toward Marsport. As the dunes dwindled behind them, Gordon could see the brief flare of the little rocket taking off.

They drove back through the night as rapidly as the truck could manage. Finally, they rolled into City Hall, down a ramp, and onto an elevator that took them three levels down. Trench climbed out and nodded in satisfaction. "That's it. Take tomorrow off, if you want, and I'll fix credit for you. But just remember you haven't seen anything. You don't know any more than our old friend Murdoch!"

He led them to another elevator, then swung back to the truck.

"Guns," Gordon said slowly. "Guns and contraband ammunition for the administration from Earth. And they must have paid half the graft they've taken for that. What the hell do they want it for?"

Izzy jerked a shoulder upwards and a twist ran across his pock-marked face. "War, what else? Gov'nor, Earth must be boiling about the election. Maybe Security's getting set to spring."

The idea of Marsport rebelling against Earth seemed ridiculous. Even with guns, they wouldn't have a chance if Earth sent a force of any strength to back Security. But it was the only explanation.

Gordon took the next day off to look for Sheila Corey, but nobody would admit having seen her.

He had seen crowds beginning to assemble all afternoon, but had paid no attention to them. Now he found the way back to Corey's blocked by a mob. Then he saw that the object of it all was the First Marsport Bank. It was only toward that that the shaking fists were raised. Gordon managed to get onto a pile of rubble where he could see over the crowd. The doors of the bank were locked shut, but men were attacking it with an improvised battering ram. As he watched, a pompous little man came to the upper window over the door and began motioning for attention. The crowd quieted almost at once, except for a single yell. "When do we get our money?"

"Please. Please." The voice reached back thinly as the bank president got his silence. "Please. It won't do you any good. Not a bit. We're broke. Not a cent left! And don't go blaming me. *I* didn't start the rush. Your friends did that. They took all the money, and now we're cleaned out. You can't—"

A rope rose from the crowd and settled around him. In a second, he was pulled down, and the crowd surged forward.

Gordon dropped from the rubble, staring at the bank. He'd played it safe this time—he'd put his money away, to make sure he'd have it!

A heavy hand fell on his shoulder, and he turned to see Mother Corey. "That's the way a panic is, cobber," the man said. "There's a run, then everything is ruined. I tried to get you when I first heard the rumor, but you were gone. And when this starts, a man has to get there first." He patted his side, where a bulge showed. "And I just made it, too."

The mob was beginning to break up now, but it was still in an ugly mood. "But what started it?"

"Rumors that Mayor Wayne got a big loan from the bank—and why not, seeing it was his bank! Nobody had to guess that he'd never pay it back, so—"

Gordon found Izzy organizing the bouncers from the joints and some of the citizens into a squad. Every joint was closed down tightly already. Gordon began organizing his own squad.

Izzy slipped over as he began to get them organized. "If we hold past midnight, we'll be set, gov'nor," he said. "They go crazy for a while, but give 'em a few hours and they stop most of it. I figure you know where all the scratch went?"

"Sure—guns from Earth! The damned fools!"

"Yeah. But not fools. Just bloody well-informed, gov'nor. Earth's sending a fleet—got official word of it. No way of telling how big, but it's coming."

It gave Gordon something to think about while they patrolled the beat. But he had enough for a time without that.

The mobs left the section alone, apparently scared off by the organized group ready and waiting for them. But every street and alley had to be kept under constant surveillance to drive out the angry, desperate men who were trying to get something to hang onto before everything collapsed. He saw stores being broken into, beyond his beat; and brawls as one drunken, crazed crowd met another. But he kept to his own territory, knowing that there was nothing he could do beyond it.

By midnight, as Izzy had promised, the people had begun to quiet down, however. The anger and hysteria were giving way to a sullen, beaten hopelessness.

Honest Izzy finally seemed satisfied to turn things over to the regular night men. Gordon waited around a while longer, but finally headed back to Mother Corey's place.

Mother Corey put a cup of steaming coffee into his hands. "You look worse than I do, cobber. Worse than even that granddaughter of mine. She was looking for you!"

"Sheila?" Gordon jerked the word out.

"Yeah. She left a note for you. I put it up in your room." Mother Corey chuckled. "Why don't you two get married and make your fighting legal?"

"Thanks for the coffee," Gordon threw back at him. He was already mounting the stairs.

He tossed his door open and found the letter on his bed.

"I'd rather go to Wayne," it said, "but I need money. If you want the rest of this, you've got until three tonight to make an offer. If you can find me, maybe I'll listen."

The torn-off front cover of the notebook accompanied the letter. But it was a quarter after three already, he was practically broke—and he had no idea where she could be found.

CHAPTER TEN
Marriage of Convenience

Bruce Gordon jerked the door open to yell for Izzy while he tucked the bit of notebook cover into his pocket. Then he stopped as something nibbled at his mind; the odor Gordon had smelled before registered. He yanked out the bit of notebook and sniffed. It hadn't been close enough for any length of time to be contaminated by Mother Corey, so the smell could only come from one place.

He checked the batteries on his suit and put it on quickly. There was no point in wearing the helmet inside the dome, but it was better than trying to rent one at the lockers. He buckled it to a strap. The knife slid into its sheath, and the gun holster snapped onto the suit. As a final thought, he picked up the stout locust stick he'd used under Murdoch.

There were no cabs outside tonight, of course. The streets were almost deserted, except for some prowler or desperation-driven drug addict. He proceeded cautiously, however, realizing that it would be just like Sheila to ambush him. But he reached the exit from the dome with no trouble.

"Special pass to leave at this hour," the guard there reminded him. "Of course, if it's urgent, pal…"

Gordon was in no mood to try bribes. He let his hand drop to the gun. "Police Sergeant Gordon, on official business," he said curtly. "Get the hell out of my way."

The guard thought it over, and reached for the release. Gordon swung back as he passed through. "And you'd better be ready to open when I come back."

He was in comparative darkness almost at once, and tonight there was no sign of the lights of patrolling cops. Then three specks of glaring blue light suddenly appeared in the sky, jerking his eyes up. They were dropping rapidly.

Rockets that flamed bright blue—military rockets! Earth was finally taking a hand!

He crouched in a hollow that had once been some kind of a basement until the ships had landed and cut off their jets. Then he stood up, blinking his eyes until they could again make out the pattern of the dim bulbs. He'd seen enough by the rocket glare to know that he was headed right. And finally the ugly half-cylinder of patched brick and metal that was the old Mother Corey's Chicken Coop showed up against the faint light.

He moved in cautiously, as silently as he could, and located the semi-secret entrance to the building without meeting anyone. Once in the tunnel that led to the building, he felt a little safer.

He removed his helmet, and strapped it to the back of his suit, out of the way. The old hall was in worse shape than before. Mother Corey had run a somewhat orderly place, with constant vigilance; Bruce Gordon could never have come into the hallway without being seen in the old days.

Then a pounding sound came from the second floor, and Gordon drew back into the denser shadows, staring upwards. A heavy voice picked up the exchange of shouts.

"You, Sheila, you come outa there! You come right out or I'm gonna blast that there door down. You open up."

Gordon was already moving up the stairs when a second voice reached him, and this one was familiar. "Jurgens don't want *you;* all he wants is this place—we got use for it. It don't belong to you, anyhow! Come out now, and we'll let you go peaceful. Or stay in there and we'll blast you out—in pieces."

It was the voice of Jurgens' henchman who had called on Mother Corey before elections. The thick voice must belong to the big ape who'd been with him.

"Come on out," the little man cried again. "You don't have a chance. We've already chased all your boarders out!"

Gordon tried to remember which steps had creaked the worst, but he wasn't too worried, if there were only two of them. Then his head projected above the top step, and he hesitated. Only the rat and the ape were standing near a heavy, closed door. But four others were lounging in the background. He lifted his foot to put it back down to a lower step, just as Sheila's muffled voice shrilled out a fog of profanity. He grinned, and then saw that he'd lifted his foot to a higher step.

There was a sharp yell from one of the men in the background and a knife sailed for him, but the aim was poor. Gordon's gun came out. Two of the men were dropping before the others could reach for their own weapons, and while the rat-faced man was just turning. The third dropped without firing, and the fourth's shot went wild. Gordon was firing rapidly, but not with such a stupid attempt at speed that he couldn't aim each shot. And at that distance, it was hard to miss.

Rat-face jerked back behind the big hulk of his partner, trying to pull a gun that seemed to be stuck; a scared man's ability to get his gun stuck in a simple holster was always amazing. The big guy simply lunged, with his hands out.

Gordon side-stepped and caught one of the arms, swinging the huge body over one hip. It sailed over the broken railing, to land on the floor below and crash through the rotten planking. He heard the man hit the basement, even while he was swinging the club in his hand toward the rat-faced man.

There was a thin, high-pitched scream as a collarbone broke. He slumped onto the floor, and began to try hitching his way down the steps. Gordon picked up the gun that had fallen out of the holster as the man fell and put it into his pouch. He considered the two, and decided they would be no menace.

"Okay, Sheila," he called out, trying to muffle his voice. "We got them all."

"Pie-Face?" Her voice was doubtful.

He considered what a man out here who went under that name might be like. "Sure, baby. Open up!"

"Wait a minute. I've got this nailed shut." There was the sound of an effort of some kind going on as she talked. "Though I ought to let you stay out there and rot. Damn it...uh!"

The door heaved open then, and she appeared in it; then she saw him, and her jaw dropped open slackly. "You!"

"Me," he agreed. "And lucky for you, Cuddles."

Her hand streaked to a gun in her belt. "Kill him!"

This time, he didn't wait to be attacked. He went for the door, knocking her aside. His knee caught the outside of her hip as she spun; she fell over, dropping the gun.

The two men in the room were both holding knives, but in the ridiculous overhand position that seems to be an ingrained stupidity of the human race, until it's taught better. A single flip of his locust club against their wrists accounted for both of the knives. He grabbed them by the hair of their heads, then, and brought the two skulls together savagely.

Sheila lay stretched out on the floor, where her head had apparently struck against the leg of a bed. Gordon shoved the bodies of the two men aside and looked down at the wreck of a man who lay on the dirty blanket. "Hello, O'Neill," he said.

The former leader of the Stonewall gang stared up at the club swinging from Gordon's wrist. "You ain't gonna beat me this time? I'm a sick man. Sick. Can't hurt nobody. Don't beat me again."

Gordon's stomach knotted sickly. Doing something under the pressure of necessity was one thing; but to see the sorry results of it later was another. "All right," he said. "Just stay there until I get away from this rat's nest and I won't hit you. I won't even touch you."

He was sure enough that it was no act on O'Neill's part; he wasn't so sure about Sheila. He checked the two men on the floor, who were still out cold. Then he stepped through the door carefully, to make sure that the big bruiser hadn't come back.

His ears barely detected the sound Sheila made as she reached for the knife of one of the men. Then it came—the faintest catch of breath. Gordon threw himself flat to the floor. She let out a scream as he saw her momentum carry her over him; she was at the edge of the rail, and starting to fall.

He caught her feet in his hands and yanked her back. There was nothing phony this time as she hit the floor.

"Just a matter of co-ordination, Cuddles," he told her. "Little girls shouldn't play with knives; they'll grow up to be old maids that way."

Fury blackened her face, but she still couldn't function. He picked her up and tossed her back into the room. From the broken mattress on the bed, he dug out a coil of wire and bound her hands and feet with it.

"Can't say I think much of your choice of companions these days," he commented, looking toward the bed where O'Neill was cowering. "It looks as if your grandfather picks them better for you."

"You filthy-minded hog! D'you think I'd—I'd—One room in the place with a decent door, and you can't see why I'd choose that room to keep Jurgens' devils back. You— You—"

He'd been searching the room, but there was no sign of the notebook there. He checked again to see that the wire was tight, and then picked up the two henchmen who were showing some signs of reviving.

"I'll watch them," a voice said from the door. Gordon snapped his head up to see Izzy standing there. He realized he'd been a lot less cautious than he'd thought.

Izzy grinned at his confusion. "I got enough out of the Mother to case the pitch," he said. "I knew I was right when I spotted the apeman carrying a guy with a bad shoulder away from here. Jurgens' punks, eh?"

"Thanks for coming. What's it going to cost me?"

"Wouldn't be honest to charge unless you asked me to convoy you, gov'nor. And if you're looking for the vixen's room, it's where you bunked before. I got around after I spotted you here."

Sheila Corey forced herself to a sitting position and spat at Izzy. "Traitor! Crooked little traitor!"

"Shut up, Sheila," Izzy said. "Your retainer ran out."

Surprisingly, she did shut up. Gordon went to the little space—and saw that Izzy was right; there was a nearly used-up lipstick, a comb, and a cracked mirror. There was also a small cloth bag containing a few scraps of clothes.

He turned the room upside down, but there was no sign of the notebook or papers from it.

He located her helmet and carried it down with him. "You're going bye-bye, Cuddles," he told her. "I'm going to put this on you and then unfasten your arms and legs. But if you start to so much as wiggle your big toe, you won't sit down for a month."

She pursed her lips hotly, but made no reply. He screwed the helmet on, and unfastened her arms. For a second, she tensed, while he waited, grinning down at her. Then she slumped back and lay quiet as he unfastened her legs.

He tossed her over his shoulder, and started down the rickety stairs.

There was a little light in the sky. Five minutes later, it was full daylight, which should have been a signal for the workers to start for their jobs. But today they were drifting out unhappily, as if already sure there would be no jobs by nightfall.

A few stared at Gordon and his burden, but most of them didn't even look up. The two men trudged along silently.

"Prisoner," he announced crisply to the guard, but there was no protest this time. They went through, and he was lucky enough to locate a broken-down tricycle cab.

Mother Corey let them in, without flickering an eyelash as he saw his granddaughter. Bruce Gordon dropped her onto her legs. "Behave yourself," he warned her as he took off his helmet, and then unfastened hers.

Mother Corey chuckled. "Very touching, cobber. You have a way with women, it seems. Too bad she had to wear a helmet, or you might have dragged her here by her hair. Ah, well, let's not talk about it here. My room is more comfortable—and private."

Inside, Sheila sat woodenly on the little sofa, pretending to see none of them. Mother Corey looked from one to the other, and then back to Gordon. "Well? You must have had some reason for bringing her here, cobber."

"I want her out of my hair, Mother," Gordon tried to explain. "I can lock her up—carrying a gun without a permit is reason enough. But I'd rather you kept her here, if you'll take the responsibility. After all, she's your granddaughter."

"So she is. That's why I wash my hands of her. I couldn't control myself at her age, couldn't control my son, and I don't intend to handle a female of my line. It looks as if you'll have to arrest her."

"Okay. Suppose I rent a room and put a good lock on it. You've got the one that connects with mine vacant."

"I run a respectable house now, Gordon," Mother Corey stated flatly. "What you do outside my place is your own business. But no women, except married ones. Can't trust 'em."

Gordon stared at the old man, but he apparently meant just what he said. "All right, Mother," he said finally. "How in hell do I marry her without any rigmarole?"

Izzy's face seemed to drop toward the floor. Sheila came up off the couch with a choking cry and leaped for the door. Mother Corey's immense arm moved out casually, sweeping her back onto the couch.

"Very convenient," the old man said. "The two of you simply fill out a form—I've got a few left from the last time—and get Izzy and me to witness it. Drop it in the mail, and you're married."

"If you think I'd marry you, you filthy—" Sheila began.

Mother Corey listened attentively. "Rich, but not very imaginative," he said thoughtfully. "But she'll learn. Izzy, I have a feeling we should let them settle their differences."

As the door shut behind them, Gordon yanked Sheila back to the couch. "Shut up!" he told her. "This isn't a game. Hell's popping here—you know that better than most people. And I'm up to my neck in it. If I've got to marry you to keep you out of my hair, I will."

Her face was pasty-white, but she bent her head, and fluttered her eyelashes up at him. "So romantic," she sighed. "You sweep me off my feet. You—Why, you—"

"Me or Trench! I can take you to him and tell him you're mixed up in Security, and that you either have papers on you or out at the Chicken Coop to prove it. He won't believe *you* if I take you in. Well?"

She looked at him a long time in silence, and there was surprise in her eyes. "You'd do it! You really would... All right; I'll sign your damned papers!"

Ten minutes later, he stood in what was now a connecting double room, watching Mother Corey nail up the hall door to the room that was to be hers. There were no windows here, and his own room had an excellent lock on it already—one he'd put on himself. Izzy came back as Mother Corey finished the door and began knocking a small panel out of the connecting door. The old man was surprisingly adept with his hands as he fitted hinges and a catch to the panel, and re-installed it so that Sheila could swing it open.

"They're married," Izzy said. "It's in the mail to the register, along with the twenty credits. Gov'nor, we're about due to report in."

Gordon nodded. "Be with you in a minute," he said as he paid Mother Corey for the materials and work. He jerked his head and the two men went out, leaving him alone with Sheila.

"I'll bring you some food tonight. And you may not have a private bath, but it beats the Chicken Coop. Here." He handed her the key to the connecting door. "It's the only key there is."

CHAPTER ELEVEN
The Sky's the Limit

All that day, the three rocket ships sat out on the field. Nobody went up to them, and nobody came from them; surprisingly, Wayne had found the courage to ignore them. But rumors were circulating wildly. Bruce Gordon felt his nerves creeping out of his skin and beginning to stand on end to test each breeze for danger.

With the credit they'd accumulated in the fund, nearly all their collection was theirs. Gordon went out to do some shopping. He stopped when his money was down to a hundred credits, hardly realizing what he was doing. When he went out, the street was going crazy.

Izzy had been waiting, and filled him in. At exactly sundown, the rocket ships had thrown down ramps, and a stream of jeeps had ridden down them and toward the south entrance to the dome. They had presented some sort of paper and forced the guard to let them through. There were about two hundred men, some of them armed. They had driven straight to the huge, barnlike Employment Bureau, had chased out the few people remaining there, and had simply taken over. Now there was a sign in front which simply said Marsport Legal Police Force Headquarters. Then the jeeps had driven back to the rockets, gone on board, and the ships had taken off.

Gordon glanced at his watch, finding it hard to believe it could have been done so quickly. But it was two hours after sundown.

Now a car with a loudspeaker on top rolled into view—a completely armored car. It stopped, and the speaker began operating.

"Citizens of Marsport! In order to protect your interests from the proven rapacity of the administration here, Earth has revoked the independent charter of Marsport. The past elections are hereby declared null and void. Your home world has appointed Marcus Gannett as mayor, with Philip Crane as chief of police. Other members of the council will be by appointment until legal elections can be held safely. The Municipal Police Force is disbanded, and the Legal Police Force is now being organized.

"All police and officers who remain loyal to the legal government will be accepted at their present grade or higher. To those who now leave the illegal Municipal Force and accept their duty with the Legal Force, there will be no question of past conduct. Nor will they suffer financially from the change!

"Banks will be reopened as rapidly as the Legal Government can extend its control, and all deposits previously made will be honored in full."

That brought a cheer from the crowd, as the sound truck moved on. Gordon saw two of the police officers nearby fingering their badges thoughtfully.

Then another truck rolled into view, and the Mayor's canned voice came over it, panting as if he'd had to rush to make the recording. He began directly:

"Martians! Earth has declared war on us. She has denied us our right to rule ourselves—a right guaranteed in our charter. We admit there have been abuses; all young civilizations make mistakes. But we've developed and grown.

"This is an old pattern, fellow Martians! England tried it on her colonies three hundred years ago. And the people rose up and demanded their right to rule themselves. They had troubles with their governments, too—and they had panics. But they won their freedom, and it made them great—so great that now that *one* nation—not all Earth, but that single nation!—is trying to do to us what she wouldn't permit to herself.

"Well, we don't have an army. But neither do they. They know the people of this world wouldn't stand for the landing of foreign—that's right, *foreign*—troops. So they're trying to steal our police force from us and use it for their war.

"Fellow Martians, they aren't going to bribe us into that! Mars has had enough. I declare us to be in a state of revolution. And since they have chosen the weapons, I declare our loyal and functioning Municipal Police Force to be *our* army. Any man who deserts will be considered a traitor. But any man who sticks will be rewarded more than he ever expected. We're going to protect our freedom.

"Let them open their banks—our banks—again. And when they have established your accounts, go in and collect the money! If they give it to you, Mars is that much richer. If they don't, you'll know they're lying.

"Let them bribe us if they like. We're going to win this war."

Gordon felt the crowd's reaction twist again, and he had to admit that Wayne had played his cards well.

But it didn't make the question of where he belonged, or what he should do, any easier. He waited until the crowd had thinned out a little and began heading toward Corey's, with Izzy moving along silently beside him, carrying half the packages.

He remembered the promise of forgiveness for all sins on joining the new Legal Force; but he'd read enough history to know that it was fine—as long as the struggle continued. Afterwards, promises grew dim...

He had no use for the present administration, but Earth had no right to take over without a formal investigation, and a chance for the people to state their choice.

Then he grimaced at himself. He was in no position to move according to right and wrong. The only question that counted was how he had the best chance to ride out the storm, and to get back to Earth and a normal life.

He was still in a brown study as he took the bundles from Izzy and dropped them on his bed. Izzy went out, and Gordon stood staring at the wall. Trench? Or the new Commissioner Crane? If Earth should win—and they had most of the power, after all—and Bruce Gordon had fought against Security, the mines of Mercury were waiting.

He picked up the stuff from his bed and started to sweep it aside before he lay down. Then he remembered at last; he knocked on the panel, until it finally opened a crack.

"Here," he told her. "Food, and some other stuff. There are some refuse bags, too. Yell when you want them removed."

She took the bundles woodenly until she came to a plastic can. Then she gasped. "Water! Two gallons!"

"There are heat tablets, and a skin tub." The salesgirl had explained how one gallon was enough in the plastic bag that served as a tub; he had his doubts. "Detergent. The whole works."

She hauled the stuff in and started to close the panel. Then she hesitated. "I suppose I should thank you, but I don't like to be told I stink so much you can't stand me in the next room!"

"Hell, I've gotten so I can stand your grandfather," he answered. "It wasn't that." The panel slammed shut.

He still hadn't solved his problem in the morning; out of habit, he put on his uniform and went across to Izzy's room. But Izzy was already gone.

Gordon fished into the pocket of his uniform for paper and a pencil to leave a note in case Izzy came back. His fingers found the half notebook cover instead. He drew it out, scowling at it, and started to crumple it. Then he stopped, staring at the piece of imitation leather and paper that wouldn't bend.

His fingers were still stiff as he began tearing off the thin covering with his knife; the paper backing peeled away easily.

Under it lay a thin metal plate that glowed faintly even in the dim light of Izzy's room! Gordon nearly dropped it. He'd seen such an identification plate once before.

The printing on it leaped at him: "This will identify the bearer, BRUCE IRVING GORDON, as a PRIME agent of the Office of Solar Security, empowered to make and execute any and all directives under the powers of this office." The printing in capitals was obviously done by hand, but with the same catalytic "ink" as the rest of the badge. Murdoch must have prepared it, hidden it in the notebook, then died before the secret could be revealed.

A knock sounded from across the hall. Gordon thrust the damning badge as deep into his pouch as he could cram it and looked out. It was Mother Corey.

"You've got a visitor—outside," he announced. "Trench. And I don't like the stench of that kind of cop in my place. Get him away, cobber, get him away!"

Gordon found Trench pacing up and down in front of the house, scowling up at it. But the ex-Marine smiled as he saw Bruce Gordon in uniform. "Good. At least some men are loyal. Had breakfast, Gordon?"

Gordon shook his head, and realized suddenly that the decision seemed to have been taken out of his hands. They crossed the street and went down half a block. "All right," he said, when the coffee began waking him. "What's the angle?"

Trench dropped the eyes that had been boring into him. "I'll have to trust you, Gordon. I've never been sure. But either you're loyal now or I can't depend on anyone being loyal."

During the night, it seemed, the Legal Force had been recruiting. Wayne, Arliss, and the rest of the administration had counted on self-interest holding most of the cops loyal to them. They'd been wrong. Legal forces already controlled about half the city.

"So?" Gordon asked. He could have told Trench that the fund was good-enough reason for most police deserting.

Trench put his coffee down and yelled for more. It was obvious he'd spent the night without sleep. "So we're going to need men with guts. Gordon, you had training under Murdoch—who knew his business. And you aren't a coward, as most of these fat fools are. I've got a proposition, straight from Wayne."

"I'm listening."

"Here." Trench threw across a platinum badge. "Take that—captain at large—and conscript any of the Municipal

Force you want, up to a hundred. Pick out any place you want, train them to handle those damned Legals the way Murdoch handled the Stonewall boys. In return, the sky's the limit. Name your own salary, once you've done the job. And no kickbacks, either!"

Gordon picked up the badge slowly and buckled it on, while a grim, satisfied smile spread over Trench's features. The problem seemed to have been solved. Gordon should have been satisfied, but he felt like Judas picking up the thirty pieces of silver. He tried to swallow them with the dregs of his coffee, and they stuck in his throat.

Comes the revolution and we'll all eat strawberries and scream!

A hubbub sounded outside, and Trench grimaced as a police whistle sounded, and a Municipal cop ran by. "We're in enemy territory," he said. "The Legals got this precinct last night. Captain Hendrix and some of his men wanted to come back with full battle equipment and chase them out. I had a hell of a time getting them to take it easy. I suppose that was some damned fool who tried to go back to his beat."

"Then you'd better look again," Gordon told him. He'd gone to the door and was peering out. Up the narrow little street was rolling a group of about seventy Municipal police and half a dozen small trucks. The men were wearing guns. And up the street a man in bright green uniform was pounding his fist up and down in emphasis as he called in over the precinct box.

"The idiot!" Trench grabbed Gordon and spun out, running toward the advancing men. "We've got to stop this. Get my car—up the street—call Arliss on the phone—under the dash. Or Wayne. I'll bring Hendrix."

Trench's system made some sense, and this business of marching as to war made none at all. Gordon grabbed the phone from under the dash. A sleepy voice answered to say that Commissioner Arliss and Mayor Wayne were sleeping. They'd had a hard night, and...

"Damn it, there's a rebellion going on!" Gordon told the man. Rebellion, rebellion! He'd meant to say revolution, but...

Trench was arguing frantically with the pompous figure of Captain Hendrix. From the other end of the street, a group of small cars appeared; and men began piling out, all in shiny green.

"Who's this?" the phone asked. When Gordon identified himself, there was a snort of disgust. "Yes, yes, congratulations. Trench was quite right; you're fully authorized. Did you call me out of bed just to check on that, young man?"

"No, I—" Then he hung up. Hendrix had dropped to his knees and fired before Trench could knock the gun from his hands.

There was no answering fire. The Legals simply came boiling down the street, equipped with long pikes with lead-weighted ends. And Hendrix came charging up, his men straggling behind him. Gordon was squarely in the middle. He considered staying in Trench's car and letting it roll past him. But he'd taken the damned badge.

"Hell," he said in disgust. He climbed out, just as the two groups met. It all had a curious feeling of unreality.

Then a man jumped for him, swinging a pike, and the feeling was suddenly gone. His hand snapped down sharply for a rock on the street. The pike whistled over his head, barely missing, and he was up, squashing the big stone into the face of the other. He jerked the pike away, kicked the man in the neck as he fell, and unsheathed his knife with the other hand.

Trench was a few feet away. The man might be a louse, but he was also a fighting machine of first order, still. He'd already captured one of the pikes. Now he grinned tightly at Gordon and began moving toward him. Gordon nodded—in a brawl such as this, two working together had a distinct advantage.

Then a yell sounded as more Legals poured down the street. One of them was obviously Izzy, wearing the same green as the others!

Gordon felt something hit his back, and instinctively fell, soaking up the blow. He managed to bend his neck and roll, coming to his feet. His knife slashed upwards, and the Legal fell—almost on top of the Security badge that had dropped from Gordon's pouch.

He jerked himself down and scooped it up, his eyes darting for Trench. He stuffed it back, ducking a blow. Then his glance fell on the entrance to Mother Corey's house—with Sheila Corey coming out of the seal!

Gordon threw himself back; he had to get to her.

He hadn't been watching as closely as he should. He saw the pike coming down and tried to duck...

He was vaguely conscious later of looking up, to see Sheila dragging him into some entrance, while Trench ran toward them. Sheila and Trench together—and the Security badge was still in his pouch!

CHAPTER TWELVE
Wife or Prisoner?

Something cold and damp against his forehead brought Gordon part way out of his unconsciousness finally. There was the softness of a bed under him and the bitter aftertaste of Migrainol on his tongue. He tried to move, but nothing happened. The drug killed pain, but only at the expense of a temporary paralysis of all voluntary motion.

There was a sudden withdrawal of the cooling touch on his forehead, and then hasty steps that went away from him, and the sound of a door closing.

Steps sounded from outside; his door opened, and there was the sound of two men crossing the room, one with the heavy shuffle of Mother Corey.

"No wonder the boys couldn't find where you'd stashed him, Mother. Must be a bloody big false section you've got in that trick mattress of yours!"

"Big enough for him and for Trench, Izzy," Mother Corey's wheezing voice agreed. "Had to be big to fit me."

"You mean you hid Trench out, too?" Izzy asked.

There was a thick chuckle and the sound of hands being rubbed together. "A respectable landlord has to protect himself, Izzy. For hiding and a convoy back, our Captain Trench gave me a paper with immunity from the Municipal Force. Used that, with a bit of my old reputation, to get your Mayor Gannett to give me the same from the Legals. Gannett didn't want Mother Corey to think the Municipals were kinder than the Legals, so you're in the only neutral territory in Marsport. Not that you deserve it."

"Lay off, Mother," Izzy said sharply. "I told you I had to do it. I take care of the side that pays my cut, and the bloody administration pulled the plug on my beat twice. Only honest thing to do was to join the Legals."

"And get your rating upped to a lieutenant," Mother Corey observed. "Without telling cobber Gordon!"

"Like I say, honesty pays, Mother—when you know how to collect. Hell, I figured Bruce would do the same. He's a right gee."

Mother Corey chuckled. "Yeah, when he forgets he's a machine. How about a game of shanks?"

The steps moved away; the door closed again. Bruce Gordon got both eyes open and managed to sit up. The effects of the drug were almost gone, but it took a straining of every nerve to reach his uniform pouch. His fingers, clumsy and uncertain, groped back and forth for a badge that wasn't there!

He heard the door open softly, but made no effort to look up. The reaction from his effort had drained him.

Fingers touched his head carefully, brushing the hair back delicately from the side of his skull. Then there was the biting sting of antiseptic, sharp enough to bring a groan from his lips. Sheila's hair fell over her face as she bent to replace his bandages.

Her eyes wandered toward his, and the scissors and bandages on her lap hit the floor as she jumped to her feet. She turned toward her room, then hesitated as he grinned crookedly at her. "Hi, Cuddles," he said flatly.

She bit her lips and turned back, while a slow flush ran over her face. Her voice was uncertain. "Hello, Bruce. You okay?"

"How long have I been like this?"

"Fifteen hours, I guess. It's almost midnight." She bent over to pick up the bandages and to finish with his head. "Are you hungry? There's some canned soup—I took the money from your pocket. Or coffee…"

"Coffee." He forced himself up again; Sheila propped the flimsy pillow behind him, then went into her room to come back with a plastic cup filled with brown liquid that passed for coffee here. It was loaded with caffeine, at least.

"Why'd you come back?" he asked suddenly. "You were anxious enough to pick the lock and get out."

"I didn't pick it—you forgot to lock it."

He couldn't remember what he'd done after he found the badge. "Okay, my mistake. But why the change of heart?"

"Because I needed a meal ticket!" she said harshly. "When I saw that Legal cop ready to take you, I had to go running out to save you. Because I don't have the iron guts to starve like a Martian!"

It rocked him back on his mental heels. He'd thought that she had been attacking him on the street; but it made more sense this way, at that.

"You're a fool!" he told her bitterly. "You bought a punched meal ticket. Right now, I probably have six death warrants out on me, and about as much chance of making a living as—"

"I'll stick to my chances. I don't have any others now." She grimaced. "You get things done. Now that you've got a wife to support, you'll support her. Just remember, it was your idea."

He'd had a lot of ideas, it seemed. "I've got a wife who's holding onto a notebook that belongs to me, then. Where is it?"

She shook her head. "I'm keeping the notebook for insurance. Blackmail, Bruce. You should understand that! And you won't find it, so don't bother looking..." She went into the other room and shut the door. There was the sound of the lock being worked, and then silence.

He stared at the door foolishly, swearing at all women; then grimaced and turned back to the chair where his uniform still lay. He could stay here fighting with her, or he could face his troubles on the outside. The whole thing hinged on Trench; unless Trench had shown the badge to others, his problem boiled down to a single man.

Gordon found one tablet of painkiller left in the bottle and swallowed it with the dregs of the coffee. He made sure his knife was in its sheath and that the gun at his side was loaded. He found his police club, checked the loop at its end, and slipped it onto his wrist.

At the door to the hall, he hesitated, staring at Sheila's room. Wife or prisoner? He turned it over in his mind, knowing that her words couldn't change the facts. But in the end, he dropped the key and half his money beside her door, along with a spare knife and one of his guns.

He went by Izzy's room without stopping; technically, the boy was an enemy to all Municipals. This might be neutral territory, but there was no use pressing it. Gordon went down the stairs and out through the seal onto the street entrance, still in the shadows.

His eyes covered the street in two quick scans. Far up, a Legal cop was passing beyond the range of the single dim light. At the other end, a pair of figures skulked along, trying the door of each house they passed. With the cops busy fighting each other, this was better pickings than outside the dome.

He saw the Legal cop move out of sight and stepped onto the street, trying to look like another petty crook on the prowl. He headed for the nearest alley, which led through the truckyard of Nick the Croop.

The entrance was in nearly complete darkness. Gordon loosened his knife and tightened his grip on the locust stick.

Suddenly a whisper of sound caught his ears. He stopped, not too quickly, and listened, but everything was still. A hundred feet farther on, and within twenty yards of the trucks, a swishing rustle reached his ears and light slashed hotly into his eyes. Hands grabbed at his arms, and a club swung down toward his knife. But the warning had been enough. Gordon's arms jerked upwards to avoid the reaching hands. His boot lifted, and the flashlight spun aside, broken and dark. With a continuous motion, he switched the knife to his left hand in a thumb-up position and brought it back. There was a grunt of pain; he stepped backwards and twisted. His hands caught the man behind, lifted across a hip, and heaved, just before the front man reached him.

The two ambushers were down in a tangled mess. There was just enough light to make out faint outlines, and Gordon brought his locust club down twice, with the hollow thud of wood on skulls.

His head was swimming in a hot maelstrom of pain, but it was quieting as his breathing returned to normal. As long as his opponents were slower or less ruthless, he could take care of himself.

The trouble, though, was that Isaiah Trench was neither slow nor squeamish.

Gordon gathered the two hoodlums under his arms and dragged them with him. He came out in the truckyard and began searching. Nick the Croop had ridden his reputation long enough to be careless, and the third truck had its key still in the lock. He threw the two into the back and struck a cautious light.

One of them was Jurgens' apelike follower, his stupid face relaxed and vacant. The other was probably also one of Jurgens' growing mob of protection racketeers. Gordon yanked out the man's wallet, but there was no identification; it held only a small sheaf of bills.

He stripped out the money—and finally put half of it back into the wallet and dropped it beside the hoodlum. Even in jail, a man had to have smokes.

He stuck to the alleys, not using the headlights, after he had locked the two in and started the electric motor. He had no clear idea of how the battles were going, but it looked as if the Seventh Precinct was still in Municipal hands.

There was no one at the side entrance to Seventh Precinct Headquarters and only two corporals on duty inside; the rest were probably out fighting the Legals, or worrying about it. One of the corporals started to stand up and halt him, but wavered at the sight of the captain's star that was still pinned to his uniform.

"Special prisoners," Gordon told him sharply. "I've got to get information to Trench—and in private!"

The corporal stuttered. Gordon knocked him out of the way with his elbow, reached for the door to Trench's private office, and yanked it open. He stepped through, drawing it shut behind him, while his eyes checked the position of his gun at his hip. Then he looked up.

There was no sign of Trench. In his place, and in the uniform of a Municipal captain, sat the heavy figure of Jurgens. "Outside!" he snapped. Then his eyes narrowed, and a stiff smile came onto his lips as he laid the pen down. "Oh, it's you, Gordon?"

"Where's Captain Trench?"

The heavy features didn't change as Jurgens chuckled. "Commissioner Trench, Gordon. It seems Arliss decided to get rid of Mayor Wayne, but didn't count on Wayne's spies being better than his. So Trench got promoted—and I got his job for loyal service in helping the Force recruit. My boys always wanted to be cops, you know."

Gordon tried to grin in return as he moved closer, slipping the heavy locust club off his wrist.

"I sent Ape and Mullins out to get in touch with you," Jurgens said. "But I guess they didn't reach you before you left."

Gordon shook his head slightly, while the nerves bunched and tingled in his neck. "They hadn't arrived when I left the house," he said truthfully enough.

Jurgens reached out for tobacco and filled a pipe. He fumbled in his pockets, as if looking for a light. "Too bad. I knew you weren't in top shape, so I figured a convoy might be handy. Well, no matter. Trench left some instructions about you, and—"

His voice was perfectly normal, but Gordon saw the hand move suddenly toward the drawer that was half-open. And the cigarette lighter was attached to the other side of the desk.

The locust stick left Gordon's hand with a snap. It cut through the air a scant eight feet, jerked to a stop against Jurgens' forehead and clattered onto the top of the desk, while Jurgens folded over, his mouth still open, his hand slumping out of the drawer. The club rolled toward Gordon, who caught it before it could reach the floor.

But Jurgens was only momentarily out. As Gordon slipped the loop over his wrist again, one of the new captain's hands groped, seeking a button on the edge of the desk.

The two corporals were at the door when Gordon threw it open, but they drew back at the sight of his drawn gun. Feet were pounding below as he found the entrance that led to the truck. He hit the seat and rammed down the throttle with his foot before he could get his hands on the wheel.

It was a full minute before sirens sounded behind him, and Nick the Croop had fast trucks. He spotted the squad car far behind, ducked through a maze of alleys, and lost it for another few precious minutes. Then a barricade lay ahead.

The truck faltered as it hit the nearly finished obstacle, and Gordon felt his stomach squash onto the wheel. He kept his foot to the floor, strewing bits of the barricade behind him, until he was beyond range of the Legal guns that were firing suddenly. Then he stopped and got out, raising his hands.

"Captain Bruce Gordon, with two prisoners—bodyguards of Captain Jurgens," he reported to the three men in bright new Legal uniform who were approaching warily. "How do I sign up with you?"

CHAPTER THIRTEEN
Arrest Mayor Wayne!

The Legal forces were shorthanded and eager for recruits. They had struck quickly, according to plans made by experts on Earth, and now controlled about half of Marsport. But it was a sprawling crescent around the central section, harder to handle than the Municipal territory. Bruce Gordon was sworn in at once.

Then he cooled his heels while the florid, paunchy ex-politician Commissioner Crane worried about his rating and repeated how corrupt Mars was and how the collection system was over—absolutely over. In the end, he was given a captain's pay and the rank of sergeant. As a favor, he was allowed to share a beat with Honest Izzy under Captain Hendrix, who had simply switched sides after losing the morning's battle.

Gordon's credits were changed to Legal scrip, and he was issued a trim-fitting green uniform. Then a surprisingly competent doctor examined his wound, rebandaged it, and sent him home for the day. The change was finished—and he felt like a grown man playing with dolls.

He walked back, watching the dull-looking people closing off their homes, as they had done at elections. Here and there, houses had been broken into during the night. There were occasional buzzes of angry conversation that cut off as he approached.

Marsport had learned to hate all cops, and a change of uniform hadn't altered that; instead, the people seemed to resent the loss of the familiar symbol of hatred.

He found Izzy and Randolph at the restaurant across from Mother Corey's. Izzy grinned suddenly at the sight of the uniform. "I knew it, gov'nor—knew it the minute I heard Jurgens was a cop. Did you make 'em give you my beat?"

He seemed genuinely pleased as Gordon nodded, and then dropped it, to point to Randolph. "Guess what, gov'nor. The Legals bought Randy's *Crusader*. Traded him an old job press and a bag of scratch for his reputation."

"You'll be late, Izzy," Randolph said quietly. Gordon suddenly realized that Randolph, like everyone else, seemed to be Izzy's friend. He watched the little man leave, and reached out for the menu. Randolph picked it out of his hand. "You've got a wife home, muckraker. You don't have to eat this filth."

Gordon got up, grimacing at the obvious dismissal. But the publisher motioned him back again.

"Yeah, the Legals want the *Crusader* for their propaganda," he said wearily. "New slogans and new uniforms, and none of them mean anything. Here!" He drew a small golden band from his little finger. "My mother's wedding ring. Give it to her—and if you tell her it came from me, I'll rip out your guts!"

He got up suddenly and hobbled out, his pinched face working. Gordon turned the ring over, puzzled. Finally he got up and headed for his room, a little surprised to find the door unlocked. Sheila opened her eyes at his uniform, but made no comment. "Food ready in ten minutes," she told him.

She'd already been shopping, and had installed the tiny cooking equipment used in half Marsport. There was also a small iron lying beside a pile of his laundered clothes. He dropped onto the bed wearily, then jerked upright as she came over to remove his boots. But there was no mockery on her face—and oddly, it felt good to him. Maybe her idea of married life was different from his.

She was sanding the dishes and putting them away when he finally remembered the ring. He studied it again, then got up and dropped it beside her. He was surprised as she fumbled it on to see that it fitted—and more surprised at the sudden realization that she was entitled to it.

She studied it under the glare of the single bulb, and then turned to her room. She was back a few seconds later with a small purse. "I got a duplicate key. Yours is in there," she said thickly. "And—something else. I guess I was going to give it to you anyway. I was afraid someone else might find it—"

He cut her off brusquely, his eyes riveted on the Security badge he'd been sure Trench had taken. "Yeah, I know. Your meal ticket was in danger. Okay, you've done your nightly duty. Now get the hell out of my room, will you?"

The week went on mechanically, while he gradually adjusted to the new angles of being a Legal. The banks were open, and deposits honored, as promised. But it was in the printing-press scrip of Legal currency, useful only through Mayor Gannett's trick Exchanges. Water went up from fourteen credits to eighty credits for a gallon of pure distilled. Other things were worse. Resentment flared, but the scrip was the only money available, and it still bound the people to the new regime.

Supplies were scarce, salt and sugar almost unavailable. Earth had cut off all shipping until the affair was settled, and nobody in the outlands would deal in scrip.

He came home the third evening to find that Sheila had managed to find space for her bunk in his room, cut off by a heavy screen, and had closed the other room to save the rent. It led to some relaxation between them, and they began talking impersonally.

Gordon watched for a sign that Trench had passed on his evidence of the murder of Murdoch, but there was none. The pressure of the beat took his mind from it. Looting had stepped up.

Izzy had co-operated—reluctantly, until Gordon was able to convince him that it was the people who paid his salary. Then he nodded. "It's a helluva roundabout way of doing things, gov'nor, but if the gees pay for protection any old way, then they're gonna get it!"

They got it. Hoodlums began moving elsewhere, toward easier pickings.

Gordon turned his entire pay over to Sheila; at current prices, it would barely keep them in food for a week. "I told you you had a punched meal ticket," he said bitterly.

"We'll live," she answered him. "I got a job today—barmaid, on your beat, where being your wife helps."

He could think of nothing to say to it; but after supper, he went to Izzy's room to arrange for a raid on Municipal territory. Such small raids were nominally on the excuse of extending the boundaries, but actually they were out-and-out looting.

He came back to find her cleaning up, and shoved her away. "Go to bed. You look beat. I'll sand these."

She started to protest, then let him take over.

They never made the looting raid. The next morning, they arrived at the Precinct house to find men milling around the bulletin board, buzzing over an announcement there. Apparently, Chief Justice Arliss had broken with the Wayne administration, and the mimeographed form was a legal ruling that Wayne was no longer Mayor, since the charter had been voided. He was charged with inciting a riot, and a warrant had been issued for his arrest.

Hendrix appeared finally. "All right, men," he shouted. "You all see it. We're going to arrest Wayne. By jingo, they can't say we ain't legal now! Every odd-numbered shield goes from every precinct. Gordon, Isaacs—you two been talking big about law and order. Here's the warrant. Take it and arrest Wayne!"

It took nearly an hour to get the plans settled, but finally they headed for the trucks that had been arriving. Most of them belonged to Nick the Croop, who had apparently decided the Legals would win.

Gordon and Izzy found the lead truck and led the way. They neared the bar where Sheila was working, and Bruce Gordon swore. She was running toward the center of the street, frantically trying to flag him down, and he barely managed to swerve around her. "Damned fool!" he muttered.

Izzy's pock-marked face soured for a second as he stared at Gordon. "The princess? She sure is."

The crew at the barricade had been alerted, and now began clearing it aside hastily, while others kept up a covering fire against the few Municipals. The trucks wheeled through, and Gordon dropped back to let scout trucks go ahead and pick off any rash enough to head for the call boxes. They couldn't prevent advance warning, but they could delay and minimize it.

They were near the big Municipal building when they came to the first real opposition, and it was obviously hastily assembled. The scouts took care of most of the trouble, though a few shots pinged against the truck Gordon was driving.

"Rifles!" Izzy commented in disgust. "They'll ruin the dome yet. Why can't they stick to knives?"

He was studying a map of the big building, picking their best entrance. Ahead, trucks formed a sort of V formation as they reached the grounds around it and began bulling their way through the groups that were trying to organize a defense. Gordon found his way cleared and shot through, emerging behind the defense and driving at full speed toward the entrance Izzy pointed out.

"Cut speed! Left sharp!" Izzy shouted. "Now, in there!"

They sliced into a small tunnel, scraping their sides where it was barely big enough for the truck. Then they reached a dead end, with just room for them to squeeze through the door of the truck and into an entrance marked with a big notice of privacy.

There was a guard beside an elevator, but Izzy's knife took care of him. They ducked around the elevator, unsure of whether it could be remotely controlled, and up a narrow flight of stairs, down a hallway, and up another flight. A Municipal corporal at the top grabbed for a warning whistle, but Gordon clipped him with a hasty rabbit punch and shoved him down the stairs. Then they were in front of an ornate door, with their weapons ready.

Izzy yanked the door open and dropped flat behind it. Bullets from a submachine gun clipped out, peppering the entrance and the door, and ricocheting down the hall. The yammering stopped, finally, and Izzy stuck his head and one arm out with a snap of his knife. Gordon leaped in, to see a Municipal dropping the machine gun.

There were about thirty cops inside, gathered around Mayor Wayne, with Trench standing at one side. The fools had obviously expected the machine gun to do all the work.

Izzy leaped for the machine gun and yanked it from dead hands, while the cops slowly began raising their arms. Wayne sat petrified, staring unbelievingly, and Gordon drew out the warrant. "Wayne, you're under arrest!"

Trench moved forward, his hands in the air, but with no mark of surprise or fear on his face. "So the bad pennies turn up. You damned fools, you should have stuck. I had big plans for you, Gordon. I've still got them, if you don't insist…"

His hands whipped down savagely toward his hips and came up sharply! Gordon spun, and the gun leaped in his hands, while the submachine gun jerked forward and clicked on an empty chamber. Trench was tumbling forward to avoid the shot, but he twitched as a bullet creased his shoulder. Then he was upright, waving empty hands at them, with the thin smile on his face deepening. He'd had no guns.

Gordon jerked around, but Wayne was already disappearing through a heavy door. And the cops were reaching for their guns. Gordon estimated the chances of escape and then leaped forward into their group, with Izzy at his side, seeking close quarters where guns wouldn't work.

Gun butts, elbows, fists, and clubs were pounding at him, while his own club lashed out savagely. In ten seconds, things began to haze over, but his arms went on mechanically, seeking the most damage they could work.

Then a heavy bellow sounded, and a seeming mountain of flesh thundered across the huge room. There was no shuffle to Mother Corey now. The huge legs pumped steadily, and the great arms were reaching out to flail aside clubs and knives. Men began spewing out of the brawl like straw from a thresher as the old man grabbed arms, legs, or whatever was handy. He had one cop in his left arm, using him as a flail against the others.

The Municipals broke. And at the first sign, Mother Corey leaped forward, dropping his flail and gathering Izzy and Gordon under his arms. He hit the heavy door with his shoulder and crashed through without breaking stride. Stairs lay there, and he took them three at a time.

He dropped them finally as they came to a side entrance. There was a sporadic firing going on there, and a knot of Municipals were clustered around a few Legals, busy with knives and clubs. Corey broke into a run again, driving straight into them and through, with Gordon and Izzy on his heels. The surprise element was enough to give them a few seconds.

Then they were around a small side building, out of danger. Sheila was holding the door of a large three-wheeler open. They ducked into it, while she grabbed the wheel.

They edged forward until they could make out the shape of the fight going on. The Legals had never quite reached the front of the building, obviously, and were now cut into sections. Corey tapped her shoulder, pointing out the rout, and she gunned the car.

They were through too fast to draw fire from the busy groups of battle-crazed men, leaping across the square and into the first side street they could find. Then she slowed, and headed for the main street back to Legal territory.

"Lucky we found a good car to steal," Mother Corey wheezed. He was puffing now, mopping rivulets of perspiration from his face. "I'm getting old, cobbers. Once I broke every strong-man record on Earth—still stand, too. But not now. Senile!"

"You didn't have to come," Izzy said.

"When my own granddaughter comes crying for help? When she finally admits she *needs* her old grandfather?"

Gordon was staring back at the straggling of trucks he could see beginning to break away. The raid was over, and the Legals had lost. Trench had tricked him.

Izzy grunted suddenly. "Gov'nor, if you're right, and the plain gees pay my salary, who's paying me to start fighting other cops? Or is it maybe that somebody isn't being exactly honest with the scratch they lift from the gees?"

"We still have to eat," Gordon said bitterly. "And to eat, we'll go on doing what we're told."

CHAPTER FOURTEEN
Full Circle

Hendrix had been wounded lightly, and was out when Gordon and Izzy reported. But the next day, they were switched to a new beat where trouble had been thickest and given twelve-hour duty—without special overtime.

Izzy considered it slowly and shook his head. "That does it, gov'nor. It ain't honest, treating us this way. If the crackle comes from the people, and these gees give everybody a skull cracking, then they're crooks. It ain't honest, and I'm too sick to work. And if that bloody doctor won't agree…"

He turned toward the dispensary. Gordon hesitated, and then swung off woodenly to take up his new beat. Apparently, his reputation had gone ahead of him, since most of the hoodlums had decided pickings would be easier on some beat where the cops had their own secret rackets to attend to, instead of head busting. But once they learned he was alone...

But the second day, two of the citizens fell into step behind him almost at once, armed with heavy clubs. Periodically during the shift, replacements took their place, making sure that he was never by himself. It surprised him even more when he saw that a couple of the men had come over from his old beat. Something began to burn inside him, but he held himself in, confining his talk to vague comments on the rumors going around.

There were enough of them, mostly based on truth. Part of Jurgens' old crowd had broken away from him and established a corner on most of the drugs available; they had secretly traded a supply to Wayne, who had become an addict, for a stock of weapons.

Gordon remembered the contraband shipment of guns, and compared it to the increase he'd noticed in weapons, and to the impossible prices the pushers were demanding. It made sense.

All kinds of supplies were low, and the outlands beyond Marsport had cut off all shipments. Scrip was useless to them, and the Legals were raiding all cargoes destined for Wayne's section. And the Municipals had imposed new taxes again.

He came back from what should have been his day off to find Izzy in uniform, waiting grimly. Behind the screen, there was a rustling of clothes, and a dress came sailing from behind it. While he stared, Sheila came out, finishing the zipping of her airsuit. She moved to a small bag and began drawing out the gun she had used and a knife. He caught her shoulders and shoved her back, pulling the weapons from her.

"Get out of my way, you damned Legal machine!" she spat.

"Easy, princess," Izzy said. "He hasn't seen it yet, I guess. Here, gov'nor!"

He picked up a copy of Randolph's new little *Truth* and pointed to the headline: SECURITY DENOUNCES RAPE OF MARSPORT!

The story was somewhat cooler than that, but not much. Randolph simply quoted what was supposed to be an official cable from Security on Earth, denouncing both governments and demanding that both immediately surrender. It listed the crimes of Wayne, then tore into the Legals as a bunch of dupes, sent by North America to foment trouble while they looted the city, and to give the Earth government an excuse for seizing military control of Marsport officially. Citizens were instructed not to co-operate; all members of either government were indicted for high treason to Security!

He crushed the paper slowly, tearing it to bits with his clenched hands; he'd swallowed the implication that the Legals *were* Security...

Then it hit him slowly, and he looked up. "Where's Randolph?"

"At his plant. At least he left for it, according to Sheila."

Gordon picked up Sheila's gun and buckled it on beside his own. She grabbed at it, but he shoved her back again. "You're staying here, Cuddles. You're supposed to be a woman now, remember!"

She was swearing hotly as they left, but made no attempt to follow. Gordon broke into a slow trot behind Izzy, until they could spot one of the few remaining cabs. He stopped it with his whistle, and dumped the passenger out unceremoniously, while Izzy gave the address.

"The damned fool opened up on the border—figured he'd circulate to both sections," Izzy said. "We'd better get out a block up and walk. And I hope we ain't *too* bloody late!"

The building was a wreck, outside; inside it was worse. Men in the Municipal uniform were working over the small job press and dumping the hand-set type from the boxes. On the floor, a single Legal cop lay under the wreckage, apparently having gotten there first and been taken care of by the later Municipals. Randolph had been sitting in a chair between two of the cops, but now he leaped up and tried to flee through the back door.

Izzy started forward, but Gordon pulled him back, as the cops reached for their weapons. The gun in his hand picked them out at quarters too close for a miss, starting with the cop who had jumped to catch Randolph. Izzy had ducked around the side, and now came back, leading the little man.

Randolph paid no attention to the dead men, nor to the bruises on his own body. He moved forward to the press, staring at it, and there were tears in his eyes as he ran his hands over the broken metal. Then he looked up at them. "Arrest or rescue?" he asked.

"Arrest!" a voice from the door said harshly, and Bruce Gordon swung to see six Legals filing in, headed by Hendrix himself. The captain nodded at Gordon. "Good work, Sergeant. By jinx, when I heard the Municipals were coming, I was scared they'd get him for sure. Crane wants to watch this guy shot in person!"

He grabbed Randolph by the arm.

"You're overlooking something, Hendrix," Gordon cut in. He had moved back toward the wall, to face the group. "If you ever look at my record, you'll find I'm an ex-newspaperman myself. This is a rescue. Tie them up, Izzy."

Hendrix was faster than Gordon had thought. He had his gun almost up before Gordon could fire. A bluish hole appeared on the man's forehead; he dropped slowly. The others made no trouble as Izzy bound them with baling wire.

"And I hope nobody finds them," he commented. "All right, Randy, I guess we're a bunch of refugees heading for the outside, and bloody lucky at that. Proves a man shouldn't have friends."

Randolph's face was still greenish-white, but he straightened and managed a feeble smile. "Not to me, Izzy. Right now I can appreciate friends. But you two better get going. I've got some unfinished business to tend to." He moved to one corner and began dragging out an old double-cylinder mimeograph. "Either of you know where I can buy stencils and ink and find some kind of a truck to haul this paper along?"

Izzy stopped and stared at the rabbity, pale little man. Then he let out a sudden yelp of laughter. "Okay, Randy, we'll find them. Gov'nor, you'd better tell my mother I'll be using the old sheets. Go on. You've got the princess to worry about. We'll be along later."

He grabbed Randolph's hand and ducked out the back before Gordon could protest.

Izzy could only have meant that they were going to hole up in Mother Corey's old Chicken Coop. Bruce Gordon had now managed to make a full circle, back to his beginnings on Mars. He'd started at the Coop with a deck of cards; now he was returning with a club.

He had counted on at least some regret from Mother Corey, however. But the old man only nodded after hearing that Randolph was safe. "Fanatics, crusaders and damned fools!" he said. He shook his head sadly and went shuffling back to his room, where two of his part-time henchmen were sitting.

Sheila had been sitting on the bunk, still in her airsuit. Now she jerked upright, then sank back with a slow flush. Her hands were trembling as she reached for a cup of coffee and handed it to him, listening to his quick report of Randolph's safety and the fact that he was going back outside the dome.

"I'm all packed," she said. "And I packed your things, too."

He shot his eyes around the room, realizing that it was practically bare, except for a few of her dresses. She followed his gaze, and shook her head. "I won't need them out there," she said. Her voice caught on that. "They'll be safe here."

"So will you, now that you've made up with the Mother," he told her. "Your meal ticket's ruined, Cuddles, and you made it clear a little while ago just where you stand. Remind me to tell you sometime how much fun it's been."

"Your mother was good with a soldering iron, wasn't she? You even look human." She bent to pick up a shoulder pack and a bag, and her face was normal when she stood up again. "You might guess that the cops would be happy to get hold of your wife now, though. Come on, it's a long walk."

He left the car beyond the gate, and they pushed through the locker room toward the smaller exit, stopping to fasten down their helmets. The guard halted them, but without any suspicion.

"Going hunting for those damned kids, eh?" he said. He stared at Sheila. "Lucky devil! All I got for a guide was an old bum. Okay, luck, Sergeant!"

It made no sense to Gordon, but he wasn't going to argue. They went through and out into the waste and slums beyond the domes, heading out until there were only the few phosphor bulbs to guide their way.

Gordon was moving cautiously, using his helmet light only occasionally, gun ready in his hand. But it was Sheila who caught the faint sound. He heard her cry out, and turned to see her crash into the stomach of a man with a half-raised stick. He went down with almost no resistance. Sheila shot the beam of her light on the thin, drawn face. "Rusty!"

"Hi, princess." He got up slowly, trying to grin. "Didn't know who it was. Sorry. Ever get that louse you were out for?"

She nodded. "Yeah, I got him. That's him—my husband! What's wrong with you, Rusty? You've lost fifty pounds, and—"

"Things are a mite tough out here, princess. No deliveries. Closed my bar, been living sort of hand to mouth, but not much mouth." His eyes bulged greedily as she dug into a bag and began to drag out the sandwiches she must have packed for the trip. But he shook his head. "I ain't so bad off. I ate something yesterday. But if you can spare something for the Kid—Hey, Kid!"

A thin boy of about sixteen crept out from behind some rubble, staring uncertainly. Then, at the sight of the food, he made a lunge, grabbed it, and hardly waited to get it through the slits of his suit before gulping it down. Rusty sat down, his lined old face breaking into a faint grin. He hesitated, but finally took some of the food.

"Shouldn't oughta. You'll need it. Umm." He swallowed slowly, as if tasting the food all the way down. "Kid can't talk. Cop caught him peddling one of Randolph's pamphlets, cut out part of his tongue. But he's all right now. Come on, Kid, hurry it up. We gotta convoy these people."

They were following a kind of road when headlights bore down on them. Gordon's hand was on his gun as they leaped for shelter, but there was no hostile move from the big truck. He studied it, trying to decide what a truck would be doing here. Then a Marspeaker-amplified voice shouted from it. "Any muckrakers there?"

"One," Gordon shouted back, and ran toward it, motioning the others to follow. He'd always objected to the nickname, but it made a good code. Randolph's frail hand came down to help them up, but a bigger paw did the actual lifting.

"Why didn't you two wait?" Mother Corey asked, his voice booming out of his Marspeaker. "I figured Izzy'd stop by first. Here, sit over there. Not much room, with my stuff and Randolph's, but it beats walking."

"What in hell brings you back?" Gordon asked.

The huge man shrugged ponderously. "A man gets tired of being respectable, cobber. And I'm getting old and sentimental about the Chicken Coop." He chuckled, rubbing his hands together. "But not so old that I can't handle a couple of guards that are stubborn about trucks, eh, Izzy?"

"Messy, but nice," Izzy agreed from the pile above them. "Tell those trained apes of yours to cut the lights, will you, Mother? Somebody must be using the Coop."

They stopped the truck before reaching the old wreck. In the few dim lights, the old building still gave off an air of mold and decay. Gordon shuddered faintly, then followed Izzy and the Mother into the semi-secret entrance.

Izzy went ahead, almost silent, with a thin strand of wire between his hands, his elbows weaving back and forth slowly to guide him. He was apparently as familiar with the garrote as the knife. But they found no guard. Izzy pressed the seal release and slid in cautiously, while the others followed.

In the beam of Gordon's torch, a single figure lay sprawled out on the floor halfway to the rickety stairs to the main house. Mother Corey grunted, and moved quickly to the coughing, battered old air machine. His fingers closed a valve equipped with a combination lock.

"They're all dead, cobbers," he wheezed. "Dead because a crook had to try his hand on a lock. Years ago, I had a flask of poison gas attached, in case a gang should ever squeeze me out."

In the filthy rooms above, Gordon found the corpses—about fifteen of them, and some former members of the Jurgens organization. He found the apelike bodyguard stretched out on a bunk, a vacant smile on his face.

A yell from the basement called him back down to where Izzy was busily going through piles of crates and boxes stacked along one wall. He was pointing to a lead-foil-covered box. "Dope! And all that other stuff's ammunition!"

He shivered, staring at the fortune in his hands. Then he grimaced and shoved the open can back in its case. He threw it back and began stacking ammunition cases in front of the dope. Gordon went out to get the others and start moving in the supplies and transferring the corpses to the truck for disposal. Randolph scurried off to start setting up his makeshift plant in the basement.

Mother Corey was staring about when they returned. "Filthy," he wailed. "A pigpen. They've ruined the Coop, cobber. Smell that air—even *I* can smell it!" He sniffed dolefully.

Mother Corey sighed again. "Well, it'll give the boys something to do," he decided. "When a man gets old, he likes a little comfort, cobber. Nice things around him…"

Gordon found what had been his old room and dumped his few things into it. Sheila watched him uncertainly, and then took possession of the next room. She came back a few minutes later, staring at the ages-old filth. "I'll be cleaning for a week," she said. "What are you going to do now, Bruce?"

He shook his head, and started back down the stairs. He hurried down into the basement where Randolph was arranging his mimeograph.

The printer listened only to the first sentence, and shook his head impatiently. "I was afraid you'd think of that, Gordon. Look, you never were a reporter—you ran a column. I've read the stuff you wrote. You killed and maimed with words. But you never dug up news that would help people, or tell them what they didn't suspect all along. And that's what I've got to have."

"Thanks!" Gordon said curtly. "Too bad Security didn't think I was as lousy a reporter as you do!"

"Okay. I'll give you a job, for one week. See what outer Marsport is like. Find what can be done, if anything, and do it if you can. Then come back and give me six columns on it. I'll pay Mother Corey for your food—and for your wife's—and if I can find one column's worth of news in it, maybe I'll give you a second week. I can't see a man's wife starve because he doesn't know how to make an honest living!"

Rusty and one of Mother Corey's men were on guard, and the others had turned in. Gordon went up the stairs and threw himself onto the bed in disgust.

"Bruce!" Sheila stood outlined in the doorway against the dim glow of a phosphor bulb. Her robe was partly open, and hunger burned in him; then, before he could lift himself, she bent over and began unfastening his boots. "You all right, Bruce? I heard you tossing around."

"I'm fine," he told her mechanically. "Just making plans for tomorrow."

He watched her turn back slowly, then lay quietly, trying not to disturb her again. Tomorrow, he thought. Tomorrow he'd find some kind of an answer; and it wouldn't be Randolph's charity.

CHAPTER FIFTEEN
Murdoch's Mantle

There were three men, each with a white circle painted on chest and left arm, talking to Mother Corey when Bruce Gordon came down the rickety steps. He stopped for a second, but there was no sign of trouble. Then the words of the thin man below reached him.

"So we figured when we found the stiffs maybe you'd come back, Mother. Damn good thing we were right. We can sure use that ammunition you found. Now, where's this Gordon fellow?"

"Here!" Gordon told the man. He'd recognized him finally as Schulberg, the little grocer from the Nineteenth Precinct.

The man swung suspiciously, then grinned weakly. There was hunger and strain on his face, but an odd authority and pride now. "I'll be doggoned. Whyn't you say he was with Murdoch?"

"They want someone to locate Ed Praeger and see about getting some food shipped in from outside, cobber," Mother Corey told him. "They got some money scraped together, but the hicks are doing no business with Marsport. You know Ed—just tell him I sent you. I'd go myself, but I'm getting too old to go chasing men out there."

"What's in it?" Gordon asked, reaching for his helmet.

There was a surprised exchange of glances from the others, but Mother Corey chuckled. "Heart like a steel trap, cobber," he said, almost approvingly. "Well, you'll be earning your keep here—yours and that granddaughter's, too. Here—you'll need directions for finding Praeger."

He handed the paper with his scrawled notes on it over to Gordon and went shuffling back. Gordon stuck it into his pouch, and followed the three. Outside, they had a truck waiting; Rusty and Corey's two henchmen were busy loading it with ammunition from the cellar.

Schulberg motioned him into the cab of the truck, and the other two climbed into the closed rear section. "All right," Gordon said, "what goes on?"

The other began explaining as he picked a way through the ruin and rubble. Murdoch had done better than Gordon had suspected; he'd laid out a program for a citizens' vigilante committee, and had drilled enough in the ruthless use of the club to keep the gangs down. Once the police were all busy inside the dome with their private war, the committee had been the only means of keeping order in the whole territory beyond. It was now extended to cover about half the area, as a voluntary police organization.

He pointed outside. It was changed; there were fewer people outside. Gordon had never seen group starvation before...

They passed a crowd around a crude gallows, and Schulberg stopped. A man was already dead and dangling. "Should turn 'em over to us cops," Schulberg said. "What's he hanged for?"

"Hoarding," a voice answered, and others supplied the few details. The dead man had been caught with a half bag of flour and part of a case of beans. Schulberg found a scrap of something and penciled the crime on it, together with a circle signature, and pinned it to the body.

"All food should be turned in," he explained to Gordon as they climbed back into the truck. "We figure community kitchens can stretch things a bit more. And we give a half extra ration to the guys who can find anything useful to do. We got enough so most people won't starve to death for another week, I guess. But you'd better get Praeger to send something, Gordon. Here, here's the scratch we scraped up."

He passed over a bag filled with a collection of small bills and coins. "We can trust you, I guess," he said dully. "Remember you with Murdoch, anyhow. And you can tell Praeger we got plenty of men looking for work, in case he can use 'em."

He pulled up to shout a report through the big Marspeaker as they passed the old building Murdoch had used as a precinct house. It now had a crude sign proclaiming it voluntary police

HQ and outland government center. Then he went on until they came to a spur of the little electric monorail system, with three abandoned service engines parked at the end.

"Extra air inside, and the best we could do for food. Was gonna try myself, but I don't know Praeger," Schulberg said. He handed over a key, and nodded toward the first service engine. "Good luck, Gordon—and damn it, we're—we gotta eat, don't we? You tell him that! It ain't much—but get what you can!"

He swung the truck, and was gone. Gordon climbed into the enclosed cab and pulled back questioningly on the only lever he could see. The engine backed briefly; he reversed the control. Then it moved forward, picking up speed. Apparently there was still power flowing in from the automatic atomic generators.

He got off to puzzle out a switch, using Mother Corey's scrawled instructions.

He had vaguely expected to see more of Mars, but for eight hours there was only the bare flatness and dunes of unending sandy surface and scraggly, useless native plants, opened out to the sun. Marsport had been located where the only vein of uranium had been found on Mars, and the growing section was closer to the equator.

Then he came to villages. Again there was the sight of children running around without helmets. He stopped once for directions, and a man stared at him suspiciously and finally threw a switch reluctantly.

He was finally forced to stop again, sure that he was near, now. This time, it was in what seemed to be a major shipping center in the heart of the lines that ran helter-skelter from village to village. Another suspicious-eyed man studied him. "You won't find Praeger on his farm—couldn't reach it in that, anyhow," he said finally. Then he turned up his Marspeaker. "Ed! Hey, Ed!"

Down the street, the seal of a building opened, and the big, bluff figure of Praeger came out. His eyes narrowed as he spotted Gordon; then he grinned and waved his visitor forward.

Inside, there was evidence of food, and a rather pretty girl brought out another platter and set it before Gordon. He ate while they exchanged uncertain, rambling information; finally, he got down to his errand.

Praeger seemed to read his mind. "I can get the stuff sent, Gordon. I'm head of the shipping committee for this quadrant. But why in hell should I? The last time, every car was looted in Outer Marsport. If they won't let us get the oil and chemicals we need, why should we feed them?"

"Ever see starvation?" Gordon asked, wishing again someone else who'd felt it could carry the message. He told about a man who'd committed suicide for his kids, not stopping as Praeger's face sickened slowly. "Hell, who wouldn't loot your trains if that's going on?"

"All right, if Mother Corey'll back up this volunteer police group. I've got kids of my own... Look, you want food, we want to ship. Get your cops to give us an escort for every shipment through to the dome, and we'll drop off one car out of four for the outlands."

Gordon sat back weakly. "Done!" he said. "Provided the first shipment carries the most we can get for the credits I brought."

"It will—we've got some stuff that's about to spoil, and we can let you have a whole train of it." He took the sack of credits and tossed it toward a drawer, uncounted. "A damned good thing Security's sending a ship. Credits won't be worth much until they get this mess straightened out."

Gordon felt the hair at the base of his neck tingle. "What makes you think Security can do anything? They haven't shown a hand yet."

"They will," Praeger said. "You guys in Marsport feed yourselves so many lies you begin to believe them. But Security took Venus—and I'm not worried here, in the long run. Don't ask me how."

His voice was a mixture of bitterness and an odd certainty. "They set Security up as a nice little debating society, Gordon, to make it easy for North America to grab the planets by doing it through that Agency. Only they got better men on it than they wanted. So far, Security has played one nation against another enough to keep any from daring to swipe power on the planets. And this latest trick folded up, too. North America figured on Marsport folding up once they got a police war started, with a bunch of chiseling profiteers as their front; they expected the citizens to yell uncle all the way back to Earth. But out here, nobody thinks of Earth as a place to yell to for help, so they missed. And now Security's got Pan-Asia and United Africa balanced against North America, so the swipe won't work. We got the dope from our southern receiver. North America's called it all a mistaken emergency measure and turned it back to Security."

"Along with how many war rockets?" Gordon asked.

"None. They never gave any real power, never will. The only strength Security's ever had comes from the fact that it always wins, somehow. Forget the crooks and crooked cops, man! Ask the people who've been getting kicked around about Security, and you'll find that even most of Marsport doesn't hate it! It's the only hope we've got of not having all the planets turned into colonial empires! You staying over, or want me to give you an engineer and drag car so you can ride back in comfort?"

Gordon stared at the room, where almost everything was a product of the planet, at Praeger, and at the girl. Here was the real Mars—the men who liked it here, who were sure of their future. "I'll take the drag car."

He found Randolph waiting in a scooter outside the precinct house after he'd reported his results. He climbed in woodenly, leaving his helmet on as he saw the broken window. "A good job," the little man said. "And news for the paper, if I ever publish it again. I came over because I wasn't much use at the Coop, and everyone else was busy."

"Doing what?" Gordon asked.

Randolph grinned crookedly. "Running Outer Marsport. The Mother's the only man everybody knows, I guess—and his word has never been broken that anyone can remember. So he's helping Schulberg make agreements with the sections the volunteers don't handle. Place is lousy with people now. Heard about Mayor Wayne?"

Gordon shook his head, not caring, but the man went on. "He must have had his supply of drugs lifted somehow. He holed up one day, until it really hit him that he couldn't get any more. Then he went gunning for Trench, with some idea Trench had swiped the stuff—so Trench is now running the Municipals. And I hear the gangs are just about in control of both sections, lately."

The Chicken Coop was filled, as Randolph had said, but he slipped in and up the stairs, leaving the news to the publisher. The place had been cleaned up more than he had expected, and there must have been new plants installed beside the blower, since the air was somewhat fresher.

He found his own room, and turned in automatically...

"Bruce?" A dim light snapped on, and he stared down at Sheila. Then he blinked. His bunk had been changed to a wider one, and she lay under the thin covering on one side. Down the center, crude stitches of heavy cord showed where she had sewed the blanket to the mattress to divide it into two sections. And in one corner, a couple of blanket sections formed a rough screen.

She caught his stare and reddened slowly. "I had to, Bruce. The Coop is full, and they needed rooms—and I couldn't tell them that—that—"

"Forget it," he told her. He dropped to his own side, with barely enough room to slide between the bed and the wall, and began dragging off his boots and uniform. She started up to help him, then jerked back, and turned her head away. "Forget all you're thinking, Cuddles. I'm still not bothering unwilling women—and I'll even close my eyes when you dress."

She sighed, and relaxed. There was a faint touch of humor in her voice then. "They called it bundling once, I think. I— Bruce, I know you don't like me, so I guess it isn't too hard for you. But...sometime...oh, damn it! Sometimes you're— nice!"

"Nice people don't get to Mars. They stay on Earth, being careful not to find out what it's like up here," he told her bitterly. For a second he hesitated, and then the account of the newsboy and his would-be killers came rushing out.

She dropped a hand onto his, nodding. "I know. The Kid—Rusty's friend—wrote down what they did to him."

Gordon grunted. He'd almost forgotten about the tongueless Kid. For a second, his thoughts churned on. Then he got up and began putting on his uniform again. Sheila frowned, staring at him, and began sliding from her side, reaching for her robe. She followed him down the creaking stairs, and to the room where Schulberg, Mother Corey, and a few others were still arguing some detail.

They looked up, and he moved forward, dragging a badge from his pouch. He slapped it down on the table in front of them. "I'm declaring myself in!" he told them coldly. "You know enough about Security badges to know they can't be forged. That one has my name on it, and rating as a Prime. Do you want to shoot me, or will you follow orders?"

Randolph picked it up, and fumbled in his pocket, drawing out a tiny badge and comparing them. He nodded. "I lost connection years ago, Gordon. But this makes you my boss."

"Then give it all the publicity you can, and tell them Security has just declared war on the whole damned dome section! Mother, I want all the dope we found!" With that—about the only supply of any size left—he could command unquestioning loyalty from every addict who hadn't already died from lack of it. Mother Corey nodded, instant understanding running over his puttylike face.

Schulberg shrugged. "After your deal with Praeger, we'd probably follow you anyhow. I don't cotton to Security, Gordon—but those devils in there are making our kids starve!"

Mother Corey heaved his bulk up slowly, wheezing, and indicated his chair at the head of the table. But Gordon shook his head. He'd made his decision. His head was emptied for the moment, and he wanted nothing more than a chance to hit the bed and forget the whole business until morning.

Sheila was staring at him as he shucked off his outer clothes mechanically and crawled under the blanket. She let the robe fall to the floor and slid into the bed without taking her eyes off him. "Is it true about Security sending a ship?" she asked at last. He nodded, and her breath caught. "What happens when they arrive, Bruce?"

She was shivering. He rolled over and patted her shoulder. "Who knows? Who cares? I'll see that they know you weren't guilty, though. Stop worrying about it."

She threw herself sideways, as far from him as she could get. Her voice was thick, muffled in the blanket. "Damn you, Bruce Gordon. I *should* have killed you!"

CHAPTER SIXTEEN
Get the Dome!

To Gordon's surprise, the publicity Randolph wrote about his being a Security Prime seemed to bring the other sections of Outer Marsport under the volunteer police control even faster. But he was too busy to worry about it. He left general co-ordination in the hands of Mother Corey, while Izzy and Schulberg ran the expanding of the police force.

Praeger arrived with the first load of food, and came storming up to him. "Why didn't you tell me you were a Security Prime! I'm grade three myself."

"And I suppose that would have meant you'd have shipped in all the food we needed free?" Gordon asked.

The other stopped to think it over. Then he laughed roughly. "Nope. You're right. The growers would starve next year if they gave it all away now. Well, we'll get in enough food this way to keep you going for a while—couple of weeks, at least."

It sounded good, and might have worked if there had been the normal food reserve, or if the other three quadrants had been willing to do as much. But while the immediate pressure of starvation was lifted, Gordon's own stomach told him that it wasn't an adequate diet. Signs of scurvy and pellagra were increasing.

Bruce Gordon whipped himself into forgetting some of that. His army was growing. Or rather, his mob. There was no sense in trying to get more than the vaguest organization.

It was the eighth day when he led them out in the early dawn. He had issued extra dope and managed a slight increase in the ration, so they made a brave showing—until they reached the dome.

There were no rifles opposed to him, as he had expected, and the guard at the gate was no heavier. But the warning had somehow been given, and both forces were ready.

Stretching north from the gate were the Municipals with members of some of the gangs; the other gangmen were with the Legals to the south. And they stood within inches of the dome, holding axes and knives.

A big Marspeaker ran out from the gate, and the voice of Gannett came over it. "Go back! If just one of you gets within ten feet of the dome or entrance, we're going to rip the dome! We'll destroy Marsport before we'll give in to a doped-up crowd of riffraff! You've got five minutes to get out of sight, before we come out with rifles and knock you off! Now beat it!"

Gordon got out of the car the Kid was driving and started toward the entrance, just as the moaning wail of the crowd behind him built up.

"You fools!" he yelled. "They're bluffing. They wouldn't dare destroy the dome! Come on!"

But already the men were evaporating. He stared at the rout, and suddenly stopped fighting the hands holding him. Beside him, the Kid was crying, making horrible sounds of it. He turned slowly back to the car, and felt it get under way. His final sight was that of the Legals and Municipals wildly scrambling for cover from each other.

Mother Corey met him, dragging him back to a small room where he dug up an impossibly precious bottle of brandy. "Drink it all, cobber. So one of your Security badges had the wrong man attached to it, and word got back. Couldn't be helped. You just ran into the sacred law of Marsport—the one they teach kids. Be bad, and the dome'll collapse. The dome made Marsport, and it's taboo!"

Gordon nodded. Maybe the old man was right. "If the dome gives them a perfect cover, why let me make a jackass of myself, Mother?" he asked numbly.

Corey shook his head, setting the heavy folds of flesh to bouncing. "Gave them something to live for here, cobber. And when you get over this, you're gonna announce new plans to try again. Yes, you are! But right now, you get yourself drunk!"

He left Gordon and the bottle. After a while, the bottle was gone. He felt number, but no better, by the time Izzy came in.

"Trench is outside in a heavy-armored car, Bruce. Says he wants to see you. Something to discuss—a proposition!"

Gordon stood up, wobbling a little, trying to think. Then he swore, and headed for his room. "Tell him to go to hell!"

He saw Izzy and Sheila leave, wondering vaguely where she had been. Through the opening in the seal, he spotted them moving toward the big car outside. Then he shrugged. He finally made the stairs and reached his bed before he passed out.

Sheila was standing over him when he finally woke. She dumped a headache powder into her palm and held it out, handing him a small glass of water. He swallowed the fast-acting drug, and sat up, trying to remember. Then he wished he couldn't.

"What did Trench want?" he asked thickly.

"He wanted to show you a badge—a Security badge made out for him," she answered. "At least he said he wanted to show you something, and it was about that size. He wouldn't talk with us much. But I remember his name in the book—"

Gordon shook his head and sat up. The book, he thought, trying to focus his thoughts. The book with all the names...

"All right, Cuddles," he said finally. "You got your meal ticket, and you've outgrown it in this mess. Now I want that damned book! I've been operating in the dark. It's time I found out how to get in touch with some of those people. Where is it?"

She shook her head. "It isn't. Bruce—I don't have it. That time I gave you the note, you didn't come when I said, and I thought you wouldn't. Then Jurgens' men broke in, and I thought they'd get it, so—so I burned it. I lied to you about using it to make you keep me."

"You burned it!" He turned it over, staring at her. "Okay, Cuddles, you burned it. You were trying to kill me then, so you burned it to keep Jurgens from getting it and putting the finger on me! Where is it, Sheila? On you?"

She backed away, biting her lips. "No, Bruce. I burned it. I don't know why. I just did! No!"

She turned toward the door as he pushed up from the bed, but his arm caught her wrist, dragging her back. She whimpered once, then shrieked faintly as his hand caught the buttons on the dress, jerking them off. Then suddenly she was a writhing, biting, scratching fury. He tightened his hand and lifted her to the bed, dropping a knee onto her throat and beginning to squeeze, while he jerked the dress and thin slip off.

She sat up as he released his knee, her hoarse voice squeezed from between her writhing lips. "Are you satisfied now, you mechanical beast! Do you still think I have it on me?"

He grinned, twisting the corners of his mouth. "You don't. Don't you know a *wife* shouldn't keep secrets from her husband? A warm-blooded, affectionate husband, to boot." He bent down, knocking aside her flailing arms, and pulled her closer to him. "Better tell your husband where the book is, Cuddles!"

She cursed and he drew her closer. He bent down, forcing her head back and setting his lips on hers.

From somewhere, wetness touched his cheek; he lifted his head and looked down. The wetness came from tears that spilled out of her eyes and ran off onto the mattress. She was making no sound, and there was no resistance, but the tears ran out, one drop seeming to trip over another.

"All right, Sheila," he said. His voice was cracked in his ears. "Another week of being a failure on this planet of failures, and I might. Go ahead and tell me I'm the same as your first husband. If I can't even keep my word to you, I can at least get out and stay out." He shook his head, waiting for her denunciation. "For your amusement, I'm going to miss having you around!"

He stood up. Something touched his hand, and he looked down to see her fingers.

"Bruce," she said faintly, "you meant it! You don't hate me any more." She rubbed her wrist across her eyes, and the ghost of a smile touched her lips. "I don't think you're a failure. And maybe—maybe I'm not. Maybe I don't have to be a failure as a woman—a wife, Bruce. I don't want you to go!"

Two worlds. One huddled under its dome, forever afraid of losing that protection and having to face the life the other led; and yet driven to work together or to perish together. The sacred dome!

And suddenly he was shaking her. "The dome! It has to be the answer! Cuddles, you broke the chain enough for me to think again! We've been blind—the whole damned planet has been blind."

She blinked and then frowned. "Bruce—"

"I'm all right! I'm just half sane instead of all insane for a change." He got up, pacing the floor as he talked.

"Look, most of the people here are Martians. They've left Earth behind, and they're meeting this planet on its own terms. And they're adapting. Third-generation children—not all, but a lot of them—are breathing the air we'd die on, and they're doing fine at it. Probably second-generation ones can keep going after we'd pass out. It's just as true out here as it is on the frontier. But Marsport has that sacred dome over it. It's still trying to be Earth. And it can't do it. It's never had a chance to adjust here, and it's afraid to try."

"Maybe," she agreed doubtfully. "But what about this part of Marsport?"

"Obvious. Here, they grow up under the shadow of it. They live in a half-world, and they have to live on the crumbs the dome tosses them. Sheila, if something happened to that dome—"

"We'd be killed," she said. "How do we do it?"

He frowned, and then grinned slowly. "Maybe not!"

They spent the rest of the night discussing it. Sometime during the discussion, she made coffee, and first Randolph, then the Kid came in for briefing. Randolph was a natural addition, and the Kid had been alternately following Gordon and Sheila around since he'd first heard they were fighting against the men who'd robbed him of his right to speak. In the end, as the night spread into day, there were more people than they felt safe with, and less than they needed.

But later, as he stood beside the dome when night had fallen again, Gordon wasn't so sure. It was huge. The fabric of it was thin, and even the webbing straps that gave it added strength were frail things. But it was strong enough to hold up the pressure of over ten pounds per square inch, and the webbing was anchored in a metal sleeve that went too high for cutting. They could rip it, but not ruin it completely; and it had to be done so that no repair could ever be made.

Under it, and anchoring it, was a concrete wall all around the city.

Izzy came back from a careful exploration. "We can work enough powder under those webbing supports, and lay the fuse wire beside the plastic ring that keeps it airtight," he reported. "But God help us, gov'nor, if any gee spots us."

They worked through the night, while Rusty went back to requisition more explosives from the dwindling supply, and while the Kid and Izzy took time off to break into a closed converter plant and find wire enough to connect the charges. But dawn caught them with less done than they had hoped. Gordon went to connect a wire and switch from the battery and coil they had installed, but jerked backwards as he saw a suspicious guard staring at him.

"Let him think we're just scouting," Randolph advised.

There were suspicious looks as the group came back to the Coop, but Mother Corey waddled over to meet them. "Did you find them, cobber?" he asked quickly, and one of his eyelids flickered.

Izzy answered before Gordon could rise to it. "Not yet, Mother. May have to go back tonight."

Gordon left them discussing the mythical search for certain supplies that Mother Corey had apparently used as an alibi for their absence from the building. Sheila started to make coffee, but he shook his head and headed for the bed. She yawned and nodded, fingering the stitches that still ran down the blanket to divide it. Then she grimaced faintly and dropped down beside him on top of the blanket. Her head hit his arm, and she seemed to be asleep almost at once.

He awoke to find Izzy shaking his shoulder. He looked down for Sheila, but she was gone. Izzy followed his eyes, and shook his head.

"The princess took off in a car three hours ago," he said. "She said it was something that had to be done, gov'nor, so I figured you'd know about it."

Gordon shrugged, and let it pass. He found the rest of the group ready, with Mother Corey wishing them better luck tonight. The Mother obviously knew something; but he kept his suspicions to himself, and gave them a cover from the others.

There was no sign of Sheila near the dome. But inside, there were guards pacing along it. Gordon spotted them first, and drew the others back. If they'd found the carefully worked-in powder...

The Kid ducked down and out of the car, worming his way around the building that concealed them. He waited for the guard to vanish, and then went crawling forward. Gordon swore, but there was no sense in two of them risking themselves, only to attract more attention. And at last the Kid came back. He ducked into the truck, nodding.

"Wire and explosive still there?" Gordon asked.

The Kid made the sound he used for assent.

It made no sense; there was no reason for the sudden vigilance inside the dome.

"We might be able to run the wire in," Izzy said doubtfully.

Gordon grunted. "And tip them off to where it is, probably. No, we'll have to do it under some kind of covering, the way I had it planned in the first place, only with one more damned complication. We'll pull another false raid on the dome. As soon as we get chased off, I'll manage to set it off while they're relaxing and laughing at us."

"It smells!" Izzy told him. "Who elected you chief martyr around here? You'll be blown up, gov'nor—and if you ain't, they'll rip you to ribbons for knocking off the dome."

Then he stopped suddenly, staring. Bruce Gordon leaned forward, with Izzy's hands grabbing for him. But he'd seen it, too.

Standing next to the dome was Trench, talking to one of the guards. And beside him stood Sheila, with one hand resting on the man's elbow!

He could feel the thickness of the silence and misery in the truck, but he pushed it away, with all the other things. "Get us back, Izzy," he ordered. "We've got to round up whatever group we can and get them back here on the double. They must be counting on our original time, so they're in no hurry to remove the powder and wiring. But we can't count on any more time."

"You're going through with it?" Randolph asked doubtfully.

"In one hour. And you might pass the word along that we're doing it to save the dome. Tell the men we just found out that Trench is losing and intends to blow it up instead of letting the Legals win."

Rumor would travel fast enough, he hoped. And it should give him a few extra seconds before his forces cracked.

He lifted the switch in his hands and stared at it. It wasn't necessary now. All he had to do was to reach the battery and drop any metal across the two terminals there—if they could get back before Trench—and Sheila—could remove the battery.

It was a period of complete fog to him, but it wasn't until his motley army reached the dome, straggling up in trucks and on foot, that he snapped into focus again. There was no sign of Sheila this time, and he didn't look for her. His whole mind was concentrated down to a single point: Get the dome!

This time, there was no scattering of Municipals and Legals. The Municipal forces were rushing up toward the dome, and surprised Legals were frantically arriving in trucks. There was the beginning of a pitched battle right at the spot where Gordon needed his own cover.

It made no sense to him, and he didn't care. He marched his men up, with the thin wailing of a banshee in his ears.

"Dome warning!" Izzy shouted in his ear. "Hear that siren, gov'nor? Means they're scared we may do it. Give me that damned switch!"

He grabbed for it, but Gordon held firmly to the copper strap. And now the men inside caught sight of the approaching force. For a second, consternation seemed to reign.

Then a huge truck with a speaker on top drove into the struggling group, and the thin whisper of unintelligible words reached Gordon. The whole development made no more sense than any part of it to him, but he saw the Municipals and Legals suddenly begin to turn as a single man to face the outside menace that had crept up on them while they were boiling into a fight.

And suddenly the Marspeaker over the entrance blasted into life. "Get back! The dome is mined! Any man comes near it, it'll blow! Get back! The dome is mined!"

By Gordon's side, a sudden gargling sound came from the Kid. His hand snaked out, caught the strap from Gordon's hand, and jerked it free. Then he was running frantically forward.

Rifles lifted inside, and shots rang out, clipping bullets through the dome. In one place it began to tear, and there was a sudden savage roar from the men around Gordon. He had started forward after the Kid, but Izzy was in front of him, holding him back.

The Kid stumbled and slid across the ground, while blood spurted out from a gash across his head, and the helmet fell into pieces. Then, with a jerk, he was up. His hand reached out, the strap hit the terminals...

And where the dome had been, a clap of thunder seemed to take visible form. The webbing straps broke, and the dome jerked upwards, twisting outwards, and then falling into ribbons. The shock wave hit Gordon, knocking him from his feet into the crowd around him.

He struggled to his feet to see helmeted men pouring out of the houses around, and other men pouring forward from his own group. The few of either police force still standing and helmeted broke into a wild run, but they had no chance! The mob had decided that they had mined and exploded the dome.

He turned back toward the Coop, sick with the death of the Kid and the violence. For once, he'd had more than his fill of it.

Then a small truck drew up, and an arm went out to draw him inside the cab. He stared into the face of Isaiah Trench. And driving the truck was Sheila.

"Your wife took a helluva chance, Gordon," Trench said heavily. "And I took quite a chance, too, to set this up so nobody could ever believe you were behind it. Getting that fight started in time, after you first showed up—oh, sure, we spotted you—was the toughest job I ever did! But I guess Sheila had the roughest end, not even knowing for sure where I stood."

Gordon stared at them slowly, not quite believing it, even though it was no crazier than anything else during the past few hours.

Trench shrugged. "I was railroaded here by Security, told to be good and they'd let me go home. A lot of men got that treatment. So when Wayne was still talking about building a perfect Marsport, I joined up. He treated me right, and I took orders. But a man gets sick of working with punks and cheap hoods; he gets sicker of killing off a planet he's learned to like. I learned to take orders, though—and I took them until Wayne tried to put a bullet through me. That ended that, and I came out to join up with you. You were soused, I hear—but your wife guessed enough to take the chance of coming to me, when she thought you were going to get yourself killed. Well, I guess you get out here."

He indicated the Coop. Gordon got down, followed by Sheila as Trench took the wheel. "What happens to you now?" Gordon asked. "They'll be blaming you for the end of the dome."

"Let them. I planned on that. Too bad Trench got torn to bits by the mob, isn't it? And it's a good thing I've always kept myself a place under a safe incognito out in the sticks. Got a wife and two kids out there that even Wayne didn't know about." He stuck out a hand. "You're like Security, Gordon. You do all the wrong things, but you get the right results. Goodbye!"

Sheila watched him go, shaking her head. "He likes you, Bruce. But he can't say it. Men!"

"Women!" Gordon answered.

Then he stiffened. Coming down through the thin air of Mars was the bright blue exhaust of a rocket. The real Security was arriving!

CHAPTER SEVENTEEN
Security Payoff

It was three days before Bruce Gordon made up his mind to hunt up Security; another four days passed after they had sent him back to wait until they received orders from Headquarters for him. There was a man coming from Earth on a second ship who would see him. They gave him a chauffeur back to the Chicken Coop, and politely indicated that it would be better if he stayed within reach.

The dome had been down a full week when he watched the last of Randolph's equipment packed onto a truck and hauled away. The little publisher was back at the *Crusader* again. Rusty was busy opening his bar, and the others were all busy. Only Gordon and Sheila were left.

He heard her coming down the old stairs, and ducked out through the private exit, snapping his helmet in place as he went through the seal. She must have sensed his desire to be left alone, since she made no attempt to follow. She'd asked no questions and hadn't even tried to convince him that he'd be sent back to Earth now.

He muttered to himself as he headed over the rubble toward the previously domed section.

Out at the spaceport, ships were dropping down from Deimos with the supplies that had been held up so long, and a long line of trucks went snaking by. Credit had been established again, and the businesses were open.

For the time being, the hoods and punks were having a tough time of it, with working papers demanded as constant identification. And while it lasted, at least, Marsport was beginning to have its face lifted. Wrecks were being broken up, with salvageable material used for newer homes. Gordon came to a row of temporary bubbles, individual dwellings built like the dome, but opaque for privacy.

As Gordon drew closer to the old foundation of the dome, the feeling around began to clarify into something halfway between what he had seen on the real frontier and what he had known as a kid in Earth's slums.

They had been lucky. The dome had exploded outwards, with only bits of it falling back; and the buildings had come through the outward explosion of the pressure with little damage. Gordon grinned wryly. Schulberg's volunteers were official, now. Izzy was acting as chief of police, Schulberg was head of the reconstruction corps, and Mother Corey was temporary Mayor of all Marsport. The old charter for Marsport from North America was dead, and the whole city was now under Security charter, like the rest of the planet. But the dozen Security men had left most of the control in the Mother's hands, and the old man was up to his fat jowls in business.

Gordon moved automatically toward the Seventh Ward. Fats' Place was still open, though the crooked tables had been removed. Gordon dropped to a stool, slipping off his helmet. He reached automatically for the glass of ether-needled beer. This time, it even tasted good to him.

"On the house, copper," Fats' voice said. The man dropped to another stool, rolling dice casually between his thumbs. "And bring out a steak, there! You look as if you could stand it—and Fats don't forget old friends!"

"Friends and other things," Gordon said, remembering his first visit here. "Maybe you should have got me that night, Fats."

The other shrugged. "That's Mars." He rolled the dice out, then picked them up again. "Guess I'll have to stick to selling meals, mostly—for a while, at least. Somebody told me you'd joined Security and got banged up trying to keep Trench from blowing up the dome. Thought you'd be in the chips!"

"That's Mars," Gordon echoed the other's comment. "Why don't you pull off the planet, Fats? You could go back to Earth, I'd guess."

The other nodded. "Yeah. I went back, about ten years ago. Spent four weeks down there. I dunno. Guess a man gets used to anything... Hell, maybe I can hire some bums to sit around and whoop it up when the ships come in, and bill this as a real old Martian den of sin! Get a barker out at the port, run special busses, charge the suckers a mint for a cheap thrill."

Gordon grinned wryly; Fats would probably make more than ever.

He finished the meal, accepted a pack of the Earth cigarettes that sold at a luxury price here, and went out into the thin air of Mars. It was almost good to get out into the filth of the slums, and be heading back to the still-standing monument of the old Chicken Coop. He headed for the private entrance out of habit, and then shrugged as he realized it was a needless precaution now. He moved up the front steps and through the battered seal.

Then he stopped. Security had finally gotten around to him, it seemed. Inside the hallway, the Security man who'd first sent him to Mars was waiting.

There was a grin on the other's face. "Hello, Gordon. Finally got our orders for you. It's Mercury!"

Bruce Gordon nodded slowly. "All right. I suppose you know I ruined the dome, was supposed to have killed Murdoch, pretended I was a Security agent..."

"You *were* one," the man said. He grinned again. "We know about Murdoch, and we know where Trench is—but he's a good citizen now, so he can stay there. We're not throwing the book at you, Bruce. Damn it, we sent you here to get results, and you got them. We sent twenty others the same way—and they failed. You were a bit drastic—that I have to admit—but we're one step closer to keeping nationalism off the planets, and that's all we care about."

"I wonder if it's worth it," Gordon said slowly.

The other shook his head. "We can't know in our lifetime. All we can do is to hope. We'll probably get this Mother Corey and Isaacs elected properly; and for a while, things will improve. But there'll be pushers as long as weak men turn to drugs, and graft as long as voters allow the thing to get out of their hands. Let's say you've shifted some of the misery around a bit, and given them a chance to do better. It's up to them to take it or lose it."

"So I get sent to Mercury?"

"You can't stay here. They'll find out too much eventually." He paused, estimating Gordon. "You *can* go back to Earth, Bruce, but you won't like it now. You're a fighter. And there's hell brewing on Mercury—worse than here. We've got permission to send you there, if you'll go. With a yellow ticket, again—but without any razzle-dazzle this time.

The only thing you'll get out of it is a chance to fight for a better chance for others some day—and a promise that there'll be more, until you get old enough to sit at a desk on Earth and fight against every bickering nation there to keep the planets clean. There's a rocket waiting to transship you to the Moon on the way to Mercury right now."

Gordon sighed. "All right. But I wish you'd tell my wife sometime that—well, that I didn't just run out on her. She's had bad luck with men."

"She already knows," the Security man said. "I've been waiting for you quite a while, you know. And I've paid her the pay we owe you from the time you began using your badge. She's out shopping!"

The car pulled up to the waiting rocket, and the Security man helped him up the steps with a perfunctory wish for good luck. Then Bruce Gordon stopped as great arms surrounded him.

Mother Corey was immaculate, though not much prettier. But his old eyes were glinting. "Did you think we'd let you go without seeing you off, cobber?" he asked. "And after I took a *bath* to celebrate? I—I—Oh, drat it, I'm getting old. Izzy, you tell him."

He grabbed Gordon's hand and waddled down the landing plank. Izzy shook his head.

"I can't say it, either, gov'nor—but some day, I'm going to have one of those badges myself. Like I always said, honesty sure pays, even if it kills you. Here!"

He followed Mother Corey, leaving behind his favorite knife and a brand-new deck of reader cards, marked exactly as the ones Gordon had first used.

Gordon dropped into his seat, while the sounds outside indicated take-off time. He had less than a hundred credits, a knife, a deck of phony cards, and a yellow ticket. Mars was leaving him what he'd brought...

She dropped into the seat very quietly, but her blouse touched his arm. In her hand was a punched ticket with the orange of Mars on top and the black of Mercury on the bottom.

"Hello, Bruce," Sheila said softly. "I've been shopping and I spent the money the man gave me. This is all I have left. Do you think it's worth it? Or should I take it back?"

He turned it over in his hands slowly, and the smile came back to his face gradually.

"You got a bargain, Cuddles," he said. "A lot better than the meal ticket you bought. Let's keep it."

THE END